ALASKA FLIGHT

A Romantic Medical Thriller

Betty Kuffel

ALASKA FLIGHT

Alaska Flight is a work of fiction. Events, setting, and characters are a work of imagination or are used fictitiously. You may recognize locations or characters similar to those in this novel, but they do not represent real places or people, nor do they suggest the events described actually occurred.

Published in the U.S.A.
Montana Sunrise Books Publisher
Copyright © 2018 by Montana Sunrise Books
Author: Betty Kuffel
Cover by Blue Heron Loft

For information contact montanasunrisebooks@gmail.com
Website: http://www.bettykuffel.com

OTHER TITLES BY AUTHOR:

Kelly McKay Medical Thrillers
Deadly Pyre – Book 1 - Seattle
Deadly Spin – Book 2 - Alaska

Eyes of a Pedophile – Detecting Child Predators

*Your Heart – Prevent & Reverse Heart Disease
in Women, Men & Children*

Modern Birth Control

Coming Soon
Fatal Feast – A Biological Thriller

Kelly McKay Medical Thriller Series:
Deadly Crosswinds – Book 3 - Montana
Deadly Gold – Book 4 - Nevada

Table of Contents

Chapter 1   Flight from Chaos

Liz Elliot looked up at a huge grizzly mount in the Anchorage air terminal. The ominous bear reminded her of danger in a new land where she knew no one. Liz retrieved her bag and boarded a hotel shuttle.

Unfamiliar scenery flashed past the window, carrying Liz through a sea of run-down trailers, businesses, high rises, and finally, to the Captain Cook Hotel. She entered the opulent lobby and waited behind three rugged young men at the registration desk. Lugging heavy frame packs and talking of climbing Denali, the trio headed to the elevator. Liz placed her credit card on the counter and spoke to a cheery woman. "I have a reservation."

"Welcome to Alaska, Liz. Our last single room is on the tenth floor. Two-hundred dollars per night plus tax."

At that price, Liz decided she wouldn't be staying long, but being downtown had advantages for a stranger on foot. "Just one night will work for me."

In a plush older room, Liz tossed her bag on a king-sized bed and parted the drapes. She looked down at a busy city street lined with tour buses and throngs of people. Across the bay toward the west, distant snowy mountains edged the earth. The mountains stood white and serene against surreal colors of purple and orange bleeding together in a brilliant sunset reflected on tidal water.

Liz closed the drapes blocking the brilliant sky, trying to stop memories of passionate Arizona sunsets she'd spent with Jack Sullivan, a medical helicopter pilot, her lover, until all that changed. Two months earlier, a fiery crash killed him and two of her cohorts. With a gnawing fear of flying twisting with waves of panic and tears, she quit her flight nursing job. Liz left the desert heat and terrible memories behind to look for ER work with both feet on the ground, in a hospital far away.

A wireless connection to the outside world tied Liz to the worried parents she'd left in Washington State, and to her friend Ann back in Red Bluff, Arizona. She emailed them and then scanned the Alaska Native Hospital website for an Anchorage nursing job.

Past ER positions had provided enough stimulation to keep Liz interested, until she'd discovered the thrill of flight nursing. Completing many advanced certifications, she learned to deliver babies, align fractures, tube airways, shock hearts, and stick needles in chests to re-inflate collapsed lungs. The training led to exhilarating work. For three years, she helped airlift people from canyons, off mountainsides, and cut them from wrecked cars. But now, a burned out emotional wreck, she fled her past and the stressful job.

When the hospital website listed no ER positions, she logged off and decided to go to the personnel office in the morning, résumé in hand. She hadn't heard back from them after submitting an online application. Liz fluffed her curly black hair and put on a little lipstick before going to the hotel restaurant on the top floor.

Elevator doors gaped open and then swallowed her, rattling closed, locking her inside. Claustrophobia set her heart pounding as the elevator crept upward.

Her first panic attack occurred in Red Bluff at Jack's funeral when she was introduced to a wife she didn't know existed. Two weeks with her parents suppressed her angst enough to press on with life. She tried to calm herself by thinking about open spaces instead of being locked in a slow-moving box.

By the time she reached the top floor, hyperventilation left her hands tingling and her throat tight.

When the doors finally parted at the elegant Crow's Nest, Liz stepped off and into the gaze of a handsome man with coal-black hair and eyes, just like Jack's. His likeness stopped her breath. He seated her at a small candlelit window table where her lonely reflection sipping Cabernet blurred by tears melted in an orange sunset.

The wine stopped her trembling.

Blackened Pacific salmon brought her thoughts back from the Tex-Mex food of Red Bluff to the realization her new life had begun.

Chapter 2 Flight into Wilderness

Liz's early-morning computer search for affordable lodging ended with a nearby Days Inn motel. She ate breakfast and read the *Anchorage Daily News* before checking out of the Captain Cook. The taxi driver waited in front of her new motel while she checked in. She stashed her sparse belongings in a second-floor room before heading out to look for a job.

East of downtown, the Chugach Mountain Range and blue sky framed the brick-and-glass Alaska Native Health Center. Liz located Human Resources where she inquired about openings for RNs in the Emergency Department. The friendly receptionist took her résumé, but Liz explained she'd completed an application online a few weeks earlier.

The receptionist picked up a phone. "I'll see if Sharon can talk to you right now."

Moments later, a slender gray-haired woman appeared and invited Liz into her office. The friendly greeting and serene mountain view calmed Liz's anxiety about an uncertain future. She'd find something to do in this beautiful country.

The HR director scanned her résumé. Before they had time to discuss potential positions, the receptionist reappeared. "I'm sorry Sharon. Tim wouldn't wait."

A young man stomped in. "You can have this job. I'm outta here on the next flight to LA."

Sharon looked askance. "You've only been here three weeks. Why are you leaving?"

"Ask Dr. Lasher. We worked sixteen hours yesterday, and he expects me to jump in the plane and fly out to a village for a woman in labor." Tim glared. "I don't do OB." The tan, muscular man, who looked more like a surfer than a nurse, handed Sharon an envelope. "Just send my check to this address."

Tim brushed past a tall blond man in the doorway dressed in jeans and a turtleneck. A tan Carhartt jacket draped over one arm. He walked in. "Sharon, I need a nurse. I see Tim quit. He wasn't a good fit for the job. Yesterday, a few mosquitoes and an outdoor toilet put him over the edge."

A smile painted Liz's face after the doctor's comment.

Sharon frowned. "What's this about an OB patient?"

Dr. Lasher sat on the edge of Sharon's desk. "The health aide in Chugalak called a few minutes ago in a panic. One of my patients just came into the clinic in preterm labor. Sal's eight and a half months along." He glanced at Liz. "I'm sorry I interrupted your meeting."

"No problem. This sounds urgent."

The doctor walked to the window, scanning the sky. "It's perfect flying weather. I could fly there in just over an hour but can't go without a nurse."

Sharon raised her eyebrows, questioning. "Liz, I have an ER job opening up soon, but if you're willing to fly out with Dr. Lasher right now, we can talk about other positions when you return."

An easy decision for Liz. "I delivered a baby in the back of a car last month, but I don't want to fly in helicopters."

After her quick response, Lasher spun from his window view, smiling. "Great. We don't use helicopters. My clinic plane is a Maule taildragger with the back seats removed to make room for medical supplies."

Flying away from Red Bluff, Liz recalled the peace she'd felt in the small plane. Turbulent winds rocked the wings and stirred up dust devils tracking across the red rock desert far below and carried her away from sadness.

Sharon handed Paul her résumé. "Take a look at this. A glowing reference from her last job came in yesterday." She turned to Liz. "You're hired. We'll sort out the details, later."

Dr. Lasher said, "Hi Liz. I'm Paul Lasher. It isn't often someone walks in with these credentials. I haven't delivered a baby in years." He extended a hand. "I'd sure appreciate it if you'd come with me."

Sharon agreed. "You qualify for many openings, including the ER, but right now we need you in Chugalak."

Paul's blue eyes lit up. "I want a nurse who doesn't mind a few mosquitoes and isn't afraid to fly." He smiled. "Tim was a newcomer, a *cheechako*, not ready for Alaska."

Sharon stood. "Don't worry about flying. Paul has a perfect flight record."

"I've been here less than a day, so I guess I'm a cheechako, too, but a few mosquitoes won't bother me."

"Good." Paul's tense features relaxed. "This is usually a traveling day-clinic, not a delivery room service."

Liz stood to leave. "I know what rural life is like on the desert and in the mountains of Washington State, but I'm ready to see my first Alaskan village."

Paul headed out the door and down a flight of cement stairs to the underground garage, with Liz close behind. He strode to a Jeep Cherokee. "The airport's only a mile away. We'll be airborne in a few minutes." They hopped in, belted and sped toward the airport with him talking nonstop about the small plane, direction of flight and what to expect on arrival.

"Tell me about the patient." Liz hoped for an easy delivery without complications.

"Sal's a healthy thirty-year-old. Third pregnancy. I don't expect problems."

"Do you have an OB kit, oxygen, and infant resuscitation equipment?"

Paul nodded. "Florry has everything ready at the clinic. We have backup equipment in the plane."

With six years of nursing behind her, three of them airborne with other adrenaline junkies, scenic medical flights with an adventuresome pilot doctor to Native villages to treat common ailments sounded like a paid vacation. As they approached the airport, Liz's heart rate increased like it had when the helicopter lifted off en route to a crash site.

Paul parked near a blue and white plane on tires as large as inflated wading pools. He opened the pilot door, removed a small card, and handed it to Liz. "Take a quick walk-around with me. I'll explain the preflight checklist as I run through it. I don't want to forget anything when we're in a hurry, like today."

Lines of small airplanes tied side by side and sitting on huge tires like Paul's plane looked like strange insects ready to take flight. The sky above the airport buzzed with small planes in the landing pattern. A few sat in a line on the ground with their propellers spinning, waiting for takeoff instructions from the tower.

Liz followed Paul, watching him untie each wing and the tail. He checked strut bolts and moved the ailerons up and down assuring smooth function. Tension furrowed his brow as he spun the prop through a few revolutions and then opened a small flap in the right cowling. "Here's where we check the oil before every flight." He unscrewed a cap and removed a metal rod glistening with oil. Paul moved the oil stick close to Liz. "See the oil film on the crosshatches?"

She guided his hand down to her eye level. His body warmth and a pleasant hint of cologne stirred her senses.

"The oil should be about one quart low, not overfilled, or it'll just blow off. This is the right level." He put the stick back in place and tightened the ring. "Don't ever fly with low oil. The engine will heat up and seize. Planes disappear in Alaska every year and are never found."

"Oh, *that's* reassuring," Liz's tone sarcastic.

"I don't mean to scare you. It's the truth, a caution." Paul opened the passenger door for Liz and held out his hand. "I'll help you in. The tundra tires make it a big step up."

Liz took his hand. "I suppose this is like mounting a horse. It's easier once you've done it a few times."

Paul held her hand as she stepped up and slid onto the seat. He loosened his grip but didn't release her hand.

She didn't want him to let go. Liz felt like she'd grabbed a live wire. The jolt locked their hands together. She looked at Paul's expression, surprised at her warm feelings for the handsome stranger in the midst of the stress of flying off to parts unknown.

Paul's eyes were soft, his voice reassuring, "I'm really a nice guy. Promise. I'll try not to scare you."

"I'll be okay if you explain what you're doing so there are no surprises."

"That's a deal. I've never met a nurse who could rescue people, stick needles in chests, and do CPR. What don't you do?"

"Scrub floors."

Paul laughed out loud. "I like to clean. So far, we're a good fit."

His fingers trailed hers and he swung the door to close it.

Her hand blocked the door. Warmth surged to her face. "Do you have a pillow for me to sit on? I'm too short to see over the panel."

Paul reached into the back seat and snatched a cushion. He helped Liz position herself. "Do your feet reach the rudder pedals?"

She tapped each one. "Just right. I feel like a child being buckled in by a parent."

"I don't mind. I like the company and sure need your help." He got in and handed her a headset. She adjusted the fit and tested the intercom.

Paul turned the key and pulled a knob, pumping it twice. "The choke blasts a little extra gas in to help start a cold engine." After two groans, the prop spun to life.

He radioed the tower and taxied into position for takeoff. Soon they were speeding along the runway, and then airborne. Paul's rapid explanations allayed her fears.

A calmness wrapped Liz like a soft blanket as the small plane climbed higher and higher before entering a gentle leftward bank, bringing two distant mountain peaks into view. "We took off to the east toward the Chugach range, now we're circling north. The taller peak is Denali, Mount McKinley. The smaller one is Foraker."

"Beautiful. I'd rather see them from the air than have to climb them like some guys I saw at the hotel last night."

Paul glanced at his copilot, pleased to see her calm demeanor. "I was raised in flatland Nebraska and have no desire to climb mountains."

She scanned the instrument panel and felt his eyes. He asked, "Can you see okay?"

"I can. Being short is a disadvantage. At least I'm taller than my mom."

Paul said joking, "She must be a midget. No offense intended."

"She's a Navajo. They're pretty short."

"With all that curly hair, you don't look Native."

"Dad's Irish. I have his blue eyes, curls, and personality."

Paul looked at the beautiful woman next to him. "A good combination, I'd say."

Jack's shadow darkened Liz's thoughts like an apparition. The dead helicopter pilot was nothing like Paul whose sunny personality blunted her heartache. Liz eased her dark thoughts into a box and closed the lid. She had to go on. Anticipation of what lay ahead on her first day of work provided the distraction she needed. Liz was entering a new world, climbing into blue skies beside an attractive stranger.

The plane climbed higher, giving her a better view of the stark contrast from the desert to an alien land of sparkling water and a green rolling country punctuated with high terrain. She turned to Paul with a smile, her first real smile since Jack's death.

His eyes twinkled. "How ya doin', little one?"

"Terrific. Do they actually pay you to do this?"

"They do." Paul dipped the right wing, creating a steep bank and giving Liz a view of the shore and inlet. "The water on your right is Knik Arm, an extension of tidal water from Cook Inlet off the Bay of Alaska." He leveled out. "From here, we follow the coastline a few miles, then head into the interior."

Liz leaned back, enjoying the sound of the motor and the thought of a new life.

Paul's voice in her headset interrupted her thoughts. "It's been an hour since Tim stormed in on you and Sharon. Almost two hours since Sal's water broke. I hope she waits for us."

"We can hope. I was thinking about what we're doing. I can't believe I'm flying again, and with someone I don't know, racing to a wilderness location for a woman in labor. This is crazy. After years in helicopters, I had decided I never wanted another flight job."

"You look calm enough. I bet you have more flight hours in helicopters than I do in fixed wings."

"I've lost track, but I'm done with helicopters."

Paul sounded surprised. "Why? From what I've heard, most people find helicopter flying addictive."

Liz struggled to explain without emotion. "About a month ago, one of our ships in Arizona crashed due to mechanical failure. It killed three of my close friends." Liz's voice trembled. She looked down, holding back tears. "Sorry. It's hard to talk about it."

Paul touched her arm. "If you didn't feel emotional, I'd think there was something wrong with you."

"I came up here to escape the memories."

"I'm so sorry for you and for their families. In your job, you've seen a lot of trauma. But no one is ever prepared when it happens to friends and family."

Liz sat up straight and squared her shoulders. "I hate looking weak. I'm serious about exploring my options in Alaska. I just don't want another helicopter job."

"I think you handle stress better than I do. With all your flight experience, have you ever wanted to become a pilot?"

She shook her head and answered rapidly. "The thought never crossed my mind. I was too busy with the patients."

Resting her feet lightly on the rudder pedals, she felt each small adjustment Paul made. She watched his movements. He appeared at ease, more comfortable in the air than on the ground. "It looks like you enjoy flying."

"I love what it does for us in Alaska, taking you places without roads where you can really see the country. On the way back to Anchorage, I'll show you a few flight maneuvers, so you can get the feel of flying it yourself."

Liz felt unsure and peered out her window at the water far below. "Okay, if you think it's a good idea." She had niggling concerns about Paul's piloting skills. "Have you been flying long?"

"Many years. I learned as a teenager. Put myself through college working as a crop duster."

"How long have you been flying for the hospital?"

"Three years. I love it, but I've had bad luck with nurses. They desert me for one reason or another. None left because of my flying."

Liz wondered about the details. "I was hoping you hadn't scared them off."

"I'm very careful. I haven't dusted crops in years, but it was good training for landing on Alaskan gravel strips. This job gives me the opportunity to explore Alaska and practice medicine at the same time."

Paul pushed in a knob, increasing engine noise. "We need to fly with higher power than usual to get there faster. I hope we make it in time." He checked the GPS. "We're still half an hour out.

Liz reviewed OB delivery procedures in her mind while watching green desolate land sliced into strange jigsaw puzzle pieces by snaking rivers pass below them. Before long, Paul reduced power and descended over a small village. Buildings sprinkled along a serpentine river almost curling back on itself near the town. He made a radio report of their location, alerting other planes of their position that might be flying in the vicinity.

Paul scanned the horizon as he spoke. "When we get to the clinic, you'll find Florry isn't like most quiet Native men and women. Even eye contact can be intrusive to some of them. I had one nurse who offended everyone with his loud voice and Southern drawl. He also threw up on every flight." Paul laughed. "He didn't last long."

"Promise I won't be offensive or get airsick."

"I'm not worried." Paul adjusted the throttle. "If you put your hands on the yoke and keep your feet on the rudder pedals, you'll feel the turns and can anticipate what I'm doing on this landing."

Liz followed his suggestions.

"I'll demonstrate a couple smooth turns and show you how easy it is before I let you take over."

With that comment, her heart rate rose. "You're a trusting soul."

Paul flew over the gravel strip before turning and landing into a light wind. "We'll have to walk to the clinic. Florry usually picks us up with her four-wheeler." He taxied off the runway and parked. Carrying medical packs, they jogged along the dirt road toward a large building at the edge of the village.

Liz asked as they ran, "Do you have any emergency childbirth guidelines for me?"

Paul shook his head. "Nope. Between the two of us, our experience covers most medical situations." He led the way up three steps into the building where loud voices met them. "Sounds like Florry's having trouble with someone."

They passed desks and a schoolroom area before entering the clinic doorway where a young Native woman lay on her side on a narrow exam table. She motioned a male away from her. "Get out of here, Ike. You're drunk. Leave. Oh, here comes another one." The sweaty woman clutched a

Native woman's hand who wedged herself in front of Ike. "You heard Sal. She wants you to leave."

The disheveled man reeked of alcohol. "It's my kid. I ain't leaving." He stumbled backward, falling against Paul.

Paul grabbed Ike's arm and pulled him toward the doorway. "Sir, I'm Dr. Lasher. Your wife wants you out of here. Leave or I will see that you're removed."

Liz went to Sal. While waiting for a contraction to subside, she introduced herself. "Hi, ladies. I'm Liz, Dr. Lasher's new nurse."

Florry introduced herself and Sal.

Liz asked, "How close are the contractions?"

Florry glanced at the wall clock. "About every two minutes. I'm glad you made it."

"Me, too. - Sal, could you turn onto your back for an exam?"

The woman rolled over slowly with Florry's help. Liz folded back a light blanket and listened to Sal's lungs and then felt her bulging belly. "How are you doing?"

"I was okay till the water broke." Sal gripped Florry's hand. "The labor pains are worse than with the other two kids. Here comes another one."

Liz pulled up the sheets and donned sterile gloves. "Florry, would you put an oxygen mask on Sal and get saline ready for Paul to start an intravenous?"

Florry let go of Sal's hand and hurried to perform her duties.

Sal groaned. She tensed and strained as the contraction accelerated. Liz watched between her legs. A patch of the baby's scalp came into view.

"Pant, Sal, pant. Let me check you. Don't push."

Paul called out, still struggling to get Ike out of the clinic. "I need help, Florry. Do you have law enforcement in the village?"

"Are you kidding? No. I called my brother on the CB. He'll drag Ike out of here."

Paul shoved the man out of the room and locked the door.

Pounding and yelling continued until Florry's brother arrived. Loud voices, scuffling and a slamming door left the clinic quiet but for Sal's gasps.

A couple minutes later, a soft knock on the door and a woman's voice called, "Florry, it's Roma. Let me in."

Paul opened the door to an attractive Native woman with a waist-length braid. "Roma, did you come to help?"

"I took Sal's kids to stay with Mom. What do you want me to do?"

Sal's wild stare of pain dissipated as a contraction eased and the baby's head was no longer visible.

Roma clasped her friend's hand.

Liz slid gloved fingers inside for the exam and asked Florry, "Have you been able to get a Doppler heartbeat?"

"It was 110 a few minutes ago."

Sal cried out, "Another one is coming! It's coming!"

Liz's fingers controlled the baby's head. "Don't push, Sal. Help me."

Sal panted, trying not to push. The next contraction stacked against the last as nature tried to propel the baby out. Then, Sal strained, pushing while Liz controlled delivery of the head to reduce vaginal tissue injury. The head popped through.

Paul stood across from Liz, watching. Her fingers swept the infant's neck. She looked up at him. "There's a loop of cord around the neck. If I can't slip it over the head, we'll have to cut it." Her fingers hooked the cord. Liz pulled gently. "It's short and tight." Sweat beaded on her forehead.

Liz's hands hurriedly maneuvered around the neck. She shook her head. "I can't slip the loop over the head." She held the loop. "Can you get a clamp around this?"

Paul fumbled a bit, but finally closed the clamp. He suctioned the infant's mouth and nose while Liz reached for the second clamp and snapped it adjacent to the first.

He handed her sterile scissors. "I rather like being the nurse."

Another contraction started within seconds of closing the second clamp. Liz said, "Sal, pant. Don't push. I have to cut the cord first. Pant."

"Hurry, Liz, hurry." Sal panted as Liz took the scissors and cut the cord between the clamps. Blood spurted when the ends separated and the cord tension around the baby's neck suddenly released.

Liz checked the neck again. "No more loops. Okay, Sal, push with the next contraction. Let's have this baby."

Contractions came fast and hard. With three pushes, first one shoulder, then the other, followed by the rest of a limp infant girl.

Roma's eyes widened at the sight of the motionless baby. She moved to block Sal's view. "You have a beautiful little girl."

Liz rushed the bluish motionless baby to a table piled with towels where Florry had set up a makeshift receiving area. Bright lights over the table provided warmth. A folded little blanket lay ready

Paul again suctioned the baby's nose and mouth with a bulb syringe. He placed a tiny mask over her face and squeezed a small bag, pushing oxygen into the lungs. At the same time, Liz briskly rubbed the newborn with a towel. Within a minute of oxygen and stimulation, the baby moved her limbs and took a few breaths. Paul continued oxygen support and Liz listened to the tiny chest. "Heart rate, 110."

Sal sat up, trying to look around Roma. "Is she alive? She's not crying."

Little arms jerked. Legs kicked. Dark eyes opened and squinted in the harsh light.

After a few more seconds, the newborn took deeper breaths and cried.

Liz took a few deep breaths herself and listened to the baby's chest again. "Her lungs are clear and heart rate is coming up. It's normal, now, up to 140." The oximeter showed ninety-six-percent. Relieved by their success after rapid lifesaving actions, Liz sat in a chair, her legs trembling as she looked up at Paul with tears in her eyes. She watched him gently examining the baby.

Florry called out. "Here comes the placenta. What do I do, now?"

Liz stood and went to Sal. "Let it come on out. Massage the uterus like this to help it contract and stop bleeding." Liz

Betty Kuffel

demonstrated the procedure and placed Florry's hands in the correct position.

Paul came to her side carrying the baby wrapped in the soft blanket and placed her in Sal's arms.

Sal peered into the tiny face. "I was so worried. Thank you. She's beautiful."

Roma cheered. "Yay! You guys are awesome. Sal did a great job, too."

Sal's finger stroked her daughter's moist black hair. "Is your full name Liz?"

Liz adjusted the baby close to Sal's breast. "It's Elizabeth."

"Liz, meet Elizabeth. Seeing her every day and saying your name will remind me how lucky I am."

The smiling doctor placed an arm around Liz. "Great job."

Elizabeth wailed until she found her mother's breast. After a few tries, the little mouth encircled a nipple and suckled.

With the crisis passed, Roma left to get the kids and bring them to meet their sister.

Chapter 3   Flight to Safety

Florry turned up the gas heater to warm the multipurpose village building. Roma dragged a small cot from the schoolroom area into the clinic for the children. After observing the baby and Sal, monitoring their vital signs and checking Sal's bleeding, Liz asked, "What do you think we should do now, Paul? They both look stable. The baby's alert and her lungs are clear." She checked her chart. "Sal's vital signs are normal, and she has little bleeding. I think they'll do fine with Florry's care."

Sal repositioned the baby and struggled to stretch her cramped arm. "We're fine." I think the bleeding is normal. I can rest as long as we keep Ike out of here and my kids are with me."

Paul noted a large bruise on Sal's upper arm. "What happened to you?"

She turned away. "You don't want to know, Doctor."

Then Paul saw her bruised forearm. "How did you hurt your arms?"

Previous conversations with Sal had raised red flags to Paul about domestic abuse, but this was the first time he'd seen injuries. "Ike?"

Sal nodded. "I've been hiding it for years. I didn't want the villagers involved with family affairs, but he's getting worse."

Liz pulled a chair up to Sal's bedside. "Seeing Ike's unruly behavior, I'm concerned about you and your children, especially with a newborn."

Paul stood behind Liz. "You can't defend yourself or your kids. I'm required by law to report it, Sal. I have no choice."

Sal bowed her head, ashamed. "My sister's been trying to get me to leave him and move to Anchorage with her. I've been thinking about it but was afraid to tell him. I tried to leave once before and he beat me. I'm afraid he'll hurt me 'n' the kids."

Paul reassured the woman. "This way, it is me doing the reporting, not you."

Sal appeared pale and sad. "Lately, when Ike goes fishing with his drinking buddies, he doesn't come back all night. When he comes home drunk, he's mean." Her strained expression eased. "Can you help me? I want to leave him."

The front door slammed, followed by running footsteps. Two young children burst in, joyful to see their new sister.

"Florry, since Liz and I will be here for a while, do you have any other patients you want us to see today?"

"I had four people scheduled for two days from now. Maybe they can come today."

Roma said, "One of them is my mom. She could come in today. What time?"

"Bring her over, now. I need to make a few calls to see what I can arrange for Sal."

Florry pointed. "The satellite phone is on my desk."

He disappeared into another room to make the calls. When Paul reappeared, he announced, "A transport plane with room for Sal and the kids will arrive in about three hours to take them to Anchorage. They'll have a baby carrier and two child seats onboard." He waved two coloring books, a couple toys and a handful of crayons at Roma, "Hope you don't mind. I borrowed these from your classroom."

"Good idea. It will keep them entertained. I cancelled school for today."

Paul handed Liz the crayons and books. She sat down on the floor with the kids. The children looked to Sal for guidance.

"It's okay. Her name is Liz. She's a nice lady. Don't worry, I'll be right here."

Liz and the kids sat on the floor coloring. Paul watched their interactions. Sal's children appeared afraid to do or say anything. Were they shy or was it the behavior typical of abused children, afraid to raise ire and endure another act of violence?

Florry washed and dressed the baby in a tiny diaper and soft flannel gown. She handed Sal the swaddled infant and lifted a CB radio from its hook on the wall. With no phone service in the village, the CB served as means of open communication to anyone who might be listening. Florry's brother answered her call. "We need you to keep Ike away from here."

He agreed.

Florry explained, "I want to get Sal and the kids on their way to Anchorage without Ike's interference. We can go get some of Sal's belongings from her house." Before they finished discussing the plans, Florry's brother arrived and announced Ike had passed out at a buddy's house.

Roma and Florry left with Sal's list of items to pack up for her and the kids. The women returned with three large plastic bags of clothing, and sandwiches for everyone,

Sal looked around the room, her face relaxed. "I can never repay you. Thanks so much. After I rest awhile, I need to go to the house to get some papers and personal things I have hidden from Ike."

Florry interrupted, "You shouldn't get up so soon."

"I'll be fine." Sal sat up in bed and dangled her legs. "I'll be ready to leave as soon as I get the papers."

Paul had Sal call her sister. After she completed the call, she said, "My sister is excited about us coming. She'll take me home after we get checked out at the hospital."

Liz entertained the children telling them about flying like a bird. They giggled, scribbling over many pages in the books. Liz hugged them. Paul had never wanted kids, but after watching Liz, he decided it wasn't such a bad idea.

Liz felt Paul's eyes on her as he walked toward them.

The children silenced as Paul neared.

Sal reassured them. "He won't hurt you. He's a nice doctor who helped me and will help you if you get sick."

The kids continued coloring, peeking looks at Paul. They moved closer to Liz when he sat down on the floor to join them. Paul leaned into Liz, smelling her fluffy hair. "You're doing a great job with the kids."

She smiled at them. "They're adorable."

The kids eyed Liz and Paul.

The little boy held a crayon in his clenched fist scribbling angrily in his coloring book. Dark eyes darted at Paul and then back at his book. "My dad bad. He hurts my mom." The clenched crayon indented the page. "I scared." A big tear rolled down his cheek. "He said he would beat my butt if I tell."

His little sister hugged him. "Don't cry. We'll fly away like a bird and be happy."

Liz thought about the trouble these children had experienced in their short years. She hoped the future would be brighter, much brighter, for them and their mother.

"The airplane will be here right after lunch." Paul added, for the children's benefit, "It's a flying bus with special seats for kids."

Liz clapped her hands. "Yay! You get to fly!"

Florry left the clinic for a while and then returned, stating she had three patients coming in right after lunch.

Liz sat on a child's chair and ate lunch at a low classroom table. Paul ate his sandwich sitting on the floor near her. Florry joined them after leaving Roma holding the baby while Sal slept. Paul said, "Tim left for LA this morning saying he wouldn't be back."

Florry laughed. "I'm glad Tim wasn't your nurse today. I think he would have fainted dead away and we'd have been taking care of him. Did I scare him too much?" She laughed. "He called me a maniac on wheels after I took him for a little ride on my four-wheeler."

Paul said, "The city boy wasn't ready for you or the Alaskan bush."

Florry asked, "How was the flight today, Liz? Bumpy?"

"We had a good flight. You'll have to do more than drive fast to scare me off."

Florry focused on Liz's face. "Are you part Native? You look like you might be."

"My mom's Navajo. She grew up in New Mexico."

"I thought so." Florry smiled. "You fit right in. I hope you like it here with us."

Paul placed his hand on Liz's arm. "She's been flying in medical helicopters for years in Arizona. This was an Alaskan baptism by fire, and she did great."

"You'll find every day up here's an adventure. I'll try to be nicer to you next time." Florry emphasized, "Alaska grows on you. People either love it or hate it."

Paul asked, "Florry, what is going on with Roma's mother?"

"I'm not sure. She has a fast heart rate and swollen legs. She'll be here as soon as Roma can leave to pick her up. I'll hold the baby, so Sal can sleep."

After eating their sandwiches, Liz settled the kids on a cot for a nap. They snuggled together beneath a blanket.

Sal awakened when Roma returned with her mother. Florry walked Sal around the clinic to be sure she was stable enough for a four-wheeler ride to her home. Village transportation was sparse, four-wheelers, snow machines or dog sleds.

Florry helped Sal dress and walked her around the clinic to test her stability before the women climbed on the 4-wheeler to pick up the important papers before leaving.

* * *

A gray-haired woman sat on a folding chair near an exam table, self-consciously adjusting her long cotton dress and pink cardigan. A blood pressure cuff and stethoscope hung on a wall hook behind her. When Paul walked in, she gave him a toothless grin.

"Hi, Vivian. Nice to see you, again." He motioned, "This is my new nurse, Liz."

Liz greeted her.

Unfazed by the stressful morning and without a hair out of place from her long French braid, Vivian's daughter, stood beside the older woman. "Welcome to the Alaskan bush, where the people are nice, and the mosquitoes are hungry." Roma's smile revealed gleaming straight teeth. "Mom's been a challenge. This might be her own fault. Sometimes she spits out her water pills because she doesn't like using the honey bucket at night."

Liz raised her eyebrows. "Hmm. What's a honey bucket?"

"An indoor biffy. A pot to pee in. Out here in the bush there's no indoor plumbing."

Paul kindly addressed the elder. "I hear you're having some trouble."

Liz wrapped the cuff around Vivian's arm. "Florry gave us some of your history." She checked her vital signs.

In a few minutes, Florry returned with Sal and joined them at Vivian's side. Liz announced her vital signs and Florry recorded them, then helped Vivian into an exam gown while Paul, Roma and Liz talked.

Paul said, "Roma left Alaska for a while, but couldn't stay away."

"I attended college in Seattle. After Dad died, I came back to be with Mom and took the job as the village teacher. It's great being home."

Vivian hung her head and said nothing. Paul helped her step up and sit on the exam table. He and Liz listened to her lungs and asked more questions. They checked pulses in her swollen legs.

Paul asked Liz, "So, what's your diagnosis?"

"Heart failure, in atrial fibrillation at a fast rate." Liz asked Florry, "Has she had atrial fib before?"

Florry shook her head. "Not sure what that is, but her heart's always been regular."

Liz examined Vivian's belly and focused on one area. "Does it hurt here?"

Vivian nodded. She looked away from Liz. "A little, not bad."

Roma glared at the old woman. "Mom, you never told me you had pain."

Paul examined Vivian's lower abdomen, first gently and then probing deeper on the left side.

Vivian moved away, trying to avoid his fingers.

Roma's brows furrowed. "She's had trouble with constipation. Could it be something worse?"

Paul nodded to Roma's question. "Vivian, you need to come into Anchorage for some tests. We will have a heart specialist examine you and get a CT scan of your belly."

Roma squeezed the old woman's hand. "How soon do we have to go?"

Paul sat down beside Vivian. "I'll adjust your medication today to slow the heart rate. Vivian, you must take the water pill. It will be about a week before we can get everything scheduled with the hospital and make arrangements for

Roma's classes." He looked at her daughter. "You could both take the mail plane to Anchorage. Would next Thursday work?"

Roma helped her mother sit up. "Fine. The kids in the village will love being out of school on Thursday and Friday, while we get Mom checked out."

Vivian dressed slowly with her daughter's help. The bent old woman hobbled out, clinging to a beautifully carved diamond willow walking stick.

Liz and Paul completed the medical records on Sal and the baby, with copies for the Anchorage physicians. The afternoon clinic patients, who had minor problems, were soon on their way.

The kids and Sal were ready when the transport aircraft landed. Liz placed the newborn in a carrier and strapped her in. Sal made sure her children were belted and ready. With the baby beside Sal, the little family flew off to a new home.

Sal waved goodbye.

After Paul, Liz, and Florry discussed medical issues, their successful resuscitation of Sal's baby and plans for the next clinic visit. Florry gave them a ride out to the airstrip.

* * *

Turbulent air over Cook Inlet on their way back rocked the small plane and sucked them into a downdraft. Paul reduced power.

Liz tightened her seat belt and assured him, "A little turbulence has never bothered me, but I don't like flying in clouds. I like to see where I'm going."

"With clear skies this afternoon, we don't have to worry about clouds."

Paul pointed out landmarks and had Liz take the controls, turning and circling. He watched her expression.

Calm, confident, controlled. Gentle turns. "Liz, you're a natural. If you like flying with me, we can go on some fun trips when I'm not working." He took the controls and skirted the busy Anchorage airspace to give Liz a view of the surrounding area before returning to Merrill Field, where he landed and tied the plane in place. "We should call Sharon and tell her you survived our first flight and saved a baby, but she leaves work at five, so she has already left." He pulled the last knot tight and placed chock blocks around the wheels. "I can drop you back at the hotel, but I hate this day to end. Could I fix you dinner?"

Liz smiled, glad he had feelings similar to hers. "It has been a great day. One to celebrate. I even have a baby named after me."

"Right. Let's stop at the grocery store on the way. I'll grill some steaks. Plus, I need a glass of good wine to celebrate after all our excitement."

Liz said, "I've been in town less than twenty-four hours. It seems much longer."

"A whirlwind arrival. Relaxing with food and wine will make a good end to your first day in Alaska."

Chapter 4   An Awakening

Liz pictured Paul's house as a woodsy bungalow on the edge of a creek. Instead, his three-level home perched high in the Rabbit Creek foothills south of town, overlooking the Anchorage Basin. The home abutted a rock wall. The lower level melded into steep terrain. They drove into a garage located on the middle level and walked into an expansive open living room with an arc of windows covering the entire west side.

The 180-degree view extended across Cook Inlet and the Bay of Alaska to the horizon, where the Alaska Range rose white and jagged against the sky. The view similar to the one from her Captain Cook Hotel room, just farther away from the saltwater shoreline.

Liz prepared the salad before joining Paul on a deck off the kitchen. A flannel shirt she found draped over a chair blunted the cool evening air.

Paul turned away from the steaks and skewers of mushrooms when she approached. "You look like a child in your daddy's coat. Are you warm enough?"

"I'm fine. I love to watch men work." She breathed in the delicious smells. "You seem to be enjoying yourself. Are you hungry like I am?"

"Starved and ready for a glass of wine. Let me flip these before we go in and pick out a bottle. I keep a few on hand." Paul led her through the kitchen and into a large pantry. He extended an arm, stopping her forward progress, and reached behind a row of canned goods on a pantry shelf to flip a switch.

A three-foot-diameter section of the floor near their feet tilted upward with a faint whir. The pantry light, shining down through an ornate spiral wrought-iron staircase, cast lacy shadows onto the floor of the wine cellar below. Along one entire wall, wine bottles lay horizontal in rows. "You didn't tell me you were a wine connoisseur."

"I'm not. This is a great wine cellar, tornado shelter, hideout, and library. Of course, we don't have tornados in Alaska, I have nothing to hide from, and I'd rather read in

natural light. I think the first owner must have been hiding
something other than expensive wine."

"Did you know him?"

"He'd already left town when I bought the house. The
real estate broker said he was a wine fanatic, but the room is
overly secure. The whole back wall is blasted into solid rock."

"Can I go down with you?"

"Sure. You'll be the first lady I've ever had in my lair."

Liz started down. "I hope you aren't a maniac disguised
as a nice doctor, or I may never be seen again." She stopped,
feeling a little claustrophobic as she descended. "I have a
question. What if the electricity goes off? Can you still open
the trapdoor?"

"I've never tried it. The worst thing that can happen is
we'll get stuck down there," he said, joking.

Liz faked concern, trying to hide her zing of panic at the
thought of being locked in the wine cellar. "I hope you have
enough wine to last."

He pointed. "I was kidding. It's easy to open. This spring
trigger raises the edge enough to get your fingers under it.
Then it opens by just pushing up. Do you want to try it?"

"No. I believe you."

Liz followed the spiral steps to the bottom. She looked
up, watching his feet clad in wool socks stepping down,
followed by long legs and a slender torso. Finally, his smiling
face emerged. Their blue eyes met.

She stepped aside in the narrow corridor to let him pass.
As he did, he placed a hand on each of her shoulders. "You're
full of surprises and smart as hell. You scare me. I've never
met a woman like you."

She wrapped her arms around him. A smile crinkled her
eyes. "I'm harmless."

"I don't believe that for a minute."

Liz smiled.

Paul turned to the wall of wine and pulled out a bottle.
"Châteauneuf-du-Pape, my favorite, a nice red. Want to try
it?"

"If it's your favorite, yes, but a cheap Cabernet
Sauvignon would do."

"I save this for special occasions. A celebration! We saved a baby's life and I met you."

"It *has* been a wild day. Let's celebrate." She wanted to say . . . "and I met you!" Instead, Liz controlled herself and looked around the room, distracted by three walls of floor-to-ceiling wine bottles. An alcove behind the circular stairway against the far wall held a futon couch with a footstool and a flat-screen TV with a DVD player. Rows of books filled a narrow bookshelf. "This is certainly a hideaway. No one would find you down here."

"That's what I meant. I wondered why the previous owner had this built. There's a tiny bathroom, a hidden refrigerator, and even a liquor cabinet inside the wall behind the bookcase. He rotated the shelves, revealing more bottles. "The guy left this cabinet stocked with some terrific booze."

Liz looked around. "I bet this place has stories we don't want to hear."

"It would be interesting to know more about the place. I wanted to ask him something about the property but couldn't locate him. I think he was using an alias."

She climbed up on the bottom step and admired her new friend. "I love it, a house of mysteries." Liz's elevation placed their faces in close proximity.

Paul pulled her to him in a playful hug, pressing the cool wine bottle against her flank.

She snuggled against him. "I'm glad I came to Alaska."

Paul enveloped her in his arms and lifted, so her toes barely touched the step.

Liz felt his firm body, alive in the right places. Paul gently lowered her back to her perch. "You aren't harmless, Liz. You're electric!" He took a deep breath.

Her cheeks flushed. She whispered, "We'd better get back to the steaks before they burn."

"It may be too late and I'm not sure I care, but I wouldn't want you to charge me with harassment."

"I wouldn't call this, *unwanted* advances." She ran up the winding stairs, all the while yearning to stay in the safe lair with him, forgetting claustrophobia, wondering why she was so drawn to Paul.

Was she ready for a relationship? She didn't want to use him to escape Jack's memory, but Jack had lied and used her.

Liz had to learn to trust again.

Paul's eyes followed her athletic body climbing the circular staircase.

As the sun dipped lower on the mountain-rimmed horizon, they talked with comfort, exploring their interests and job details. They sat side-by-side in the dining area facing the setting sun. After finishing the salad and overdone steak, Paul poured each of them another glass of wine. He acted comfortable, yet Liz sensed a tension the wine hadn't softened.

They sipped until the sky turned black, leaving nothing but a flickering candle inside for light. In the distance, stars sparkled bright, competing with strobes on jets landing at Anchorage International.

Liz wondered about Paul's subdued behavior. "You're awfully quiet. Are you tired? Do you want to take me home?"

"It's been a long day, but I still don't want it to end. That baby would have died without you. I don't think I could have saved her."

"Luck was on our side. Plus, we got Sal and the kids to a safer environment."

"You did a wonderful job with the kids. I watched you. You're a natural."

Liz joked, hoping to lighten his spirit. "I've practiced with dogs."

"I'd have a dog if I didn't work so much. The past two years . . ." Paul stopped, thought a moment, and then continued. ". . . have been tough on me. Sharon is the only one who really knows what happened."

Liz didn't know what to say. She worried about what might be coming next. Did someone die? What?

Paul's voice shook. "My wife left me for *my nurse,* a woman. I found them naked in our bed."

Liz's gut clenched. "I'm sorry. It's difficult to recover from betrayal."

Paul studied his hands. "Never wanted to work with another woman. Sharon hired male nurses for the job with me." He looked at Liz. "I can't believe I'm telling you this. Meeting you today changed those bitter feelings."

Liz's eyes sparkled in the candlelight. "Did I break a spell?"

"It's been a magical day. I better get you home before I say something I regret."

She put her arm around his shoulder.

Paul continued, "Don't feel sorry for me. I feel like a weight has lifted. Even if you don't take the job with me, I'd love to teach you to fly."

"Will you be at the hospital tomorrow morning?"

He nodded.

"Could we meet for coffee?"

"I'll do better than that. Let's have a free breakfast in the doctors' lounge. After that, I'm have a bush clinic. I'd love to have you join me."

Paul drove Liz to the entrance of Days Inn. He opened her door and extended his hand.

She took his hand in both of hers. "Thanks for the great food and wine, for not scaring me in the sky, and for being willing to work with a girl nurse."

He squeezed her hand. "I hope it's just the beginning. Goodnight, Liz."

Warm feelings toward the interesting doctor surged as she walked away from his car to the motel entrance. Liz waved as he drove off.

Chapter 5   ER Crisis

In the morning, Sharon reviewed potential positions with Liz and set her up in a cubicle to watch a mandatory training video for new employees. Minutes later, she returned. "I called Dan Eaton, the ER nursing director to give you a tour this morning. His night nurse is in the OR having gallbladder surgery. Could you fill in and orient to the ER tonight?"

Liz stopped the video. "Paul and I were going to fly out to visit some of his friends this morning. Working ER tonight would help me decide if I'd rather work there or with Paul in the bush clinics. I'll do it."

Sharon said, "Great. Thanks."

After finishing the video, Liz went into Sharon's office. She hung up the receiver. "Dan just said he'd work the night with you. There will be one additional registered nurse, plus someone in triage."

Paul returned after his meeting and learned of the change. "Darn, I was hoping you'd go with me. You could meet Rollie and Vera on our way back. It would give you a good taste of what life in Alaska is like. We'll have to do that later."

He dropped Liz off at the Days Inn on his way to Merrill Field. She hung out in her room, read a newspaper and took a long afternoon nap, knowing she'd be up all night. After a light dinner at a nearby restaurant, a cab dropped her off at the ER.

The ambulance doors whooshed open. She entered and looked around. Dan met her. "You must be Liz Elliot. Thanks so much for working. I'll take you to the locker room where you can change into scrubs." He handed her a name tag. "The ER's calm right now, so I can show you around."

She returned to the desk in baggy scrubs, the color of her eyes. An ER doc sat dictating. Upon seeing Liz, he clicked the hold key. "Dan told me we'd have a new nurse starting tonight." The youngish man smiled and examined Liz's left hand. "He didn't say she was good looking and single."

Dan glowered. "Mick, those comments can get you into trouble for harassment."

The doctor stood up and extended his hand. "I'll watch my manners. I'm Mick Fuller." He read her ID. "Pleased to meet you, Miss Liz."

She cringed at the thought of working with the man.

Dan introduced her to other staff members and walked through the treatment rooms. He was reviewing radio protocols just as an en route ambulance called in. "We're Code 3 with an unstable cardiac." A siren wailed in the background. "Forty-year-old male with chest pain and hypotension. Saline running wide open. Two minutes out."

"ANMC copies. We'll meet you at the door."

Liz's mind flashed back to the night of the Arizona helicopter crash. She blocked the thoughts and her racing heart, by focusing on Dan's explanation of ER procedures, angry that her brain cycled back to the night the helicopter fell out of the sky.

Dan explained, "This is our largest room. We like it for unstable medical patients and big traumas. With all your experience, a cardiac will be easy."

She reviewed the crash cart with its cardiac emergency drugs and the operation of the defibrillator before going outside to meet the ambulance.

The siren cut a few seconds before the vehicle roared into the driveway. A medic flung open the back doors. "He's having the big one." The paramedic moved the stretcher out with their help and gave his report as they wheeled the patient inside. "Had pain all day. Worsened ten minutes before his wife called 9-1-1. Has ST-segment elevation and a weak pulse."

The overweight patient reeked of cigarette smoke. His frightened eyes stared up at Dan. "I need help. Thought it was indigestion, but it got worse. I didn't want to come in."

Liz guided the stretcher into the large treatment room. "I'm glad your wife called the ambulance. Let's get you over on the bed and start treatment."

A medic adjusted the man's oxygen mask and helped lift him to the ER bed. "His pressure was too low to give nitro. Oxygen and a saline bolus helped reduce his pain."

Another ER nurse arrived to help. Dan called for a stat electrocardiogram.

Liz introduced herself and asked the patient. "What's your name?"

The pale, sweaty man grimaced. "Chris Jensen."

In seconds, Liz connected the hospital heart monitor, drew blood for labs and started a second IV. She asked Chris his health history and watched the cardiac rhythm on the screen over his head. The monitor showed an erratic tracing with multiple abnormal wide beats. Her eyes met Dan's.

He nodded, acknowledging her concern.

Liz checked the blood pressure. "How bad is your pain, Chris?"

"No sharp pain. Pressure, like someone sitting on my chest."

Liz stood next to the tech, reading the 12-lead ECG tracing as it printed. "It's an anterior infarct."

Dan headed for the door. "I'll get Dr. Fuller in here and call the cardiac cath lab. They might still be here. Let's hope so."

Liz started interventions, aspirin, saline and rechecked his blood pressure. The saline had raised Chris's pressure enough to allow nitroglycerine. She placed a tiny tablet beneath his tongue to dilate the coronary arteries. Her calm explanations appeared to comfort the ill man. "Aspirin's a common drug used for many problems, but in your case, we will want you to take a dose, because your chest pain is from a narrowed heart artery. It can be a wonder drug to help block clotting."

Chris's breathing and oxygen level remained acceptable. No monitors alarmed but Liz's internal alarms went off with the screen showing increased spurts of wide abnormal beats due to reduced blood flow.

Dan came back. "Cardiology's in house. The cath team is en route."

Liz looked around. "Where's Mick?"

"On the phone trying to find his replacement. Rocky hasn't shown up and Mick is pissed off. His date is waiting."

Liz tensed. "We need to start a nitro drip and give him morphine."

"Just do it. We can't wait for Mick."

She spiked an intravenous line into a premixed bottle of nitroglycerine and started the infusion, hoping the continuously dripping drug would relax the diseased artery, reducing the pain and possibly decreasing heart damage.

A few minutes after the infusion started, Liz asked Chris, "How are you doing?"

"Bad. Really bad . . ." Suddenly he clutched his chest. "I'm gonna die."

Liz felt his carotid pulse while watching the monitor.

Chris's eyes rolled back, and monitor alarms sounded.

Liz said, "V-tach! He's in V-tach!"

Dan pushed the code button on the wall to summon more help and opened the emergency cart. He handed defibrillator patches to Liz. While she placed them on Chris's chest, Dan connected the wire leads to the defibrillator. He charged the machine to deliver a jolt to correct the lethal heart rhythm.

The monitor continued to show wide zigzag electrical complexes marching across the screen as the alarm screamed.

Dan ordered, "Clear! Everybody, clear!"

Staff members stepped away from the bed.

Dan pressed the defib button, sending an electrical charge through Chris's body and heart in an attempt to normalize the rhythm.

Watching the monitor, Liz said, "No change. Recharge."

The resuscitation team gathered at the bedside but stayed clear to avoid a shock from touching the bed when another defibrillation jolt surged through Chris.

Dan's voice announced, "Rhythm. He's got a slow rhythm. Check his blood pressure." Just then a gray-haired man entered. Dan greeted him. "Dr. Kellen, glad you're here. He just had a V-tach arrest. We got his rhythm back seconds ago after two shocks. It's an anterior infarct."

Dr. Kellen unlocked the ER bed and pulled it toward the door. "Let's get him to the cath lab. Let's go."

Dan placed a portable monitor/defibrillator on the foot of the bed. The team moved the bed with monitors, oxygen and IV drips going, rushing beside Dr. Kellen, who talked to the patient en route.

Liz readied a syringe of atropine to speed the heartbeat. "Dr. Kellen, his rate's in the 40s and systolic pressure is 78. I'd like to give him a milligram of atropine."

He looked at Liz. "Give it. Who are you?"

Liz injected the atropine as she walked beside the stretcher. "Liz Elliot, a new nurse."

Dan told the cardiologist. "Sorry I didn't introduce her. Liz is a flight nurse from Arizona with lots of experience who'll be covering some ER shifts."

"Helluva way to treat a new employee, Dan."

Liz watched the heart monitor as they turned into the cath lab. "The rate is up to 60."

Chris groaned as the team moved him onto the cath table.

Dr. Kellen said, "Okay, we can take it from here. Go back and save more lives. Good job."

Back in ER, the scene had turned chaotic. Medics rushed in with an unresponsive man. Liz and Dan followed them into a room, Mick Fuller in the lead. Dan spoke into Liz's ear. "Meet Rocky, the ER physician who didn't show up for work."

Mick screamed, "I need some goddamned help in here. Give me a hand getting the tube in."

Dan opened an intubation kit and handed it to Mick. Liz took over bagging oxygen into Rocky.

The medics stood back. "Do you need us?"

Mick scowled. "No. Thanks for bringing him in. Remember patient confidentiality."

The medics nodded and left. Once Mick had placed the endotracheal tube, Liz managed the tube and oxygen administration. Dan called a respiratory therapist to bring a ventilator to ER. He said to Mick, "I'll call to get an ICU bed, and for an internist to take over once he's stabilized."

"No. I'm calling Buck Sabo. It's our director's call. Maybe we can detox Rocky in the ER and keep it off the record."

Liz looked shocked by the unethical off-the-record plan.

Dan shook his head. "I want no part of an off-the-record treatment. Buck may lose his job this time, but I'm not losing my job or license."

Mick snarled, "It's hard to get doctors up here, Dan. Put a "Do Not Enter" sign on the door. Once we get him stabilized, he'll need a spin dry and another three months in a chemical detox unit." Mick regulated the ventilator cycle, rhythmically pushing oxygen into Rocky's lungs. "The stupid son of a bitch had everything going for him. His wife found out he'd been screwing around and filed divorce papers on him today."

"I'm not surprised." Dan noted to Liz, "His judgment hasn't been the best when it came to women."

Mick looked sad. "He's brilliant, but Rocky has demons."

Liz wondered what the statement meant. She monitored the vent and the comatose over-dosed ER doctor and provided one-on-one care until other arrangements could be made.

Mick stormed out of Rocky's room, furious and exhausted after working more than twelve hours with no replacement in sight.

Like a robotic reptile, the ventilator sighed and hissed in the otherwise silent room. Liz and Dan stood across from each other at the bedside. He recorded Rocky's vital signs. "His heart rate is too fast, but blood pressure is holding at 90/60."

She ran another electrocardiogram and checked Rocky's heart tracing. "We need to know what he took other than alcohol. He could develop a long QT syndrome or other cardiac toxicity."

Dan picked up the wall phone. "I'll order a drug screen and blood alcohol level. Mick probably has the empty med bottles." The door closed behind Dan, leaving Liz looking at an attractive male in his forties. His medical license and future looking bleak. Moments later, Dan returned, his face red, neck veins bulging. "Damn it, Liz. We're in a helluva mess. Medics brought in an empty bottle of two milligram lorazepam, sixty tablets. There was an empty fifth of vodka on the floor by Rocky's bed when his wife found him."

Liz studied the ECG. "This ECG looks okay, but that sedative combination could be lethal."

"That's not all. The name on the bottle isn't Rocky's. It belonged to a guy with a bag of drugs that medics transported here yesterday when Rocky was working."

"So, Rocky stole the guy's meds?"

Dan paced. "Exactly. It's an intentional mixed drug ingestion of major proportions, and Mick was trying to hide it from us."

"What is going on with Mick? This is crazy."

"He's trying to hide Rocky's mental instability from Administration. Mick grabbed the pill bottle out of my hand when I told him Rocky stole it from a patient."

Liz listened to Rocky's chest. "His lungs sound good, but we should get an X-ray to check tube placement. If he took someone else's drugs, that's drug diversion. He'll be in big trouble with the DEA and lose his ability to prescribe narcotics. Let's ask Mick about trying Romazicon to reverse the sedative effect."

"Good idea, Liz. I've seen it work fast. We could get him off the vent sooner."

"It will be safe if Rocky doesn't use sedatives on a regular basis. Otherwise, we'll be dealing with seizures from rapid withdrawal."

Dan left the room and returned with Romazicon. "Mick said to give it."

Liz pushed a small amount and continued to watch Rocky's vital signs. "How soon can we move him to ICU?"

"Mick called Buck Sabo. The ER medical director wants to keep this quiet."

Trapped in a dangerous, unethical situation, Liz worried about losing her nursing license. "That's ridiculous."

"They've known Rocky has a drinking problem and covered for him in the past. Buck is with Mick on keeping this off the record."

Liz clenched her fists, trying to control her anger. "I don't like it."

"This puts us in jeopardy." Dan closed the door. "It's bullshit! Let's see what goes down when Buck gets here, but I'm ready to call Administration."

Liz considered calling Paul to discuss the situation. "The bottom line is Rocky is a sick man and needs help."

Dan said in disgust. "We could both lose our nursing licenses. I can tell you right now. I'm not lying to anyone about this incident. I've never smelled alcohol on him at work. I hope the lab hurries with the drug screen and BA."

He called the lab. "The report already printed out in ER."

Dan left to get the report and check on the rest of the busy department. Liz monitored Rocky, making a detailed ER record and looked up when the door opened. "His blood alcohol is 0.42. A lethal level unless you practice a lot and have significant tolerance."

"Right. Combined with the large sedative drug dose, it's a clear-cut suicide attempt. Has he worked here long?"

"Six months. He's Buck's buddy from Texas. They're both cowboy types, always pushing the limits."

"I'll run another ECG in a few minutes. So far, he's tachycardic but shows no other abnormalities." Liz commented, "Too bad we can't do something to speed the metabolism of his alcohol load. I'll turn up his infusion. That might help."

Dan agreed. The door swung shut behind him. When he returned, another angry male stomped in. He took one look at Rocky. "That stupid bastard really fucked up this time." He stared at Liz, "Who the hell is this?"

"I'm Liz Elliot, a new nurse."

Buck glared. "She's an outsider and a liability. Get her out of here." His eyes stabbed Liz, "Don't you say anything to anyone about this patient. This is a gag order. Get it?" He stepped toward Liz, threatening her.

Dan stepped between them. "What do you think you're doing, Buck? I need her help. Rocky's in deep kimchi. Could have died. We have him stabilized. I need to move him to ICU."

"Get out, both of you! I'll take care of Rocky myself." Buck jerked the door open.

Dan's six-foot frame steeled against the verbal assault. He slammed the door. "You have no authority to gag us or tell us to leave."

"I'm director and can do anything I want. Get out."

Dan picked up the wall phone. "Page Administration to the ER stat. Yes, ER stat."

Buck grabbed the phone from Dan's hand and shoved him against the wall.

Betty Kuffel

Shocked by the violence, Liz edged toward the door. She tried to tell Buck about Rocky's condition, that she'd just pushed an IV dose of Romazicon to reverse the effect of the Lorazepam.

He cut her off. "If I want your help, I'll ask for it."

Chapter 6   Job in Jeopardy

The two RNs left the room. Dan dialed the on-call administrator directly and got Walt Connelly, the CEO. "Yes. I need you to come in immediately and handle a crisis. . . . No, I can't tell you over the phone. This is a crisis and you need to be here."

Mick heard Dan's final words just before he placed the receiver down. "Dan, come over here to the office and talk to me."

Dan stood staunchly. "Not without a witness. Liz, will you join me?"

Mick slammed the door behind them. "Okay. I want you both to understand we are only doing this to help one of our own. Rocky was depressed. He needs our help—your help, too. He made a bad decision. It could have killed him. We do not want this on his record."

Dan and Liz said nothing in response to Mick's comments. But Dan asked, "Where's the rest of your group?"

"Left town for a medical conference in Las Vegas. Phillips went to Fairbanks. He is returning tonight and is scheduled at 7 a.m."

Mick stood with his back against the door and looked from one to the other. "Do not tell anyone about Rocky. If the word gets out, I'll know it was you and there'll be hell to pay."

"You're threatening us." Dan stepped forward. "I'll tell Walt Connelly as soon as he arrives. Get away from the door."

Mick snarled and stepped aside. "I'll have your jobs. We all have to get back out here and take care of the patients. I'll be working twenty-four hours because there's no replacement."

The nurses pushed past Mick.

* * *

The ambulance doors parted when CEO Walt Connelly approached. He strode into the ER and looked around, confused. Buck's loud voice penetrated the closed door. "Rocky. Settle down. You'll be alright."

Dan pulled Walt into a small office and signaled Liz to join them. Before Liz closed the door behind her, Dan spewed, "Rocky is on ventilator support. He was supposed to relieve Mick but overdosed on a patient's drugs and was brought in unconscious."

Liz added, "He should be admitted to ICU, but Buck Sabo is trying to hide it from everyone and is treating him in the ER." Walt's face turned livid. He grabbed the door handle to leave, but Dan stopped him. "Buck threatened me and Liz, then placed a gag order on us. That's when I called you. We're filing harassment claims with HR in the morning against both Buck and Mick."

Liz stepped away from the door. "This situation needs to be on the record for our protection."

Walt flung open the door and stormed into Rocky's room. The door closed, but his words were clear. "Buck, what the hell is going on in here?"

The rest of the night sped by with little time for Liz and Dan to talk. She took assignments and efficiently processed the many patients, documenting everything and when Buck took over Rocky's care, Mick went back to his ER duties.

Dan took Liz aside and cautioned her. "Take no verbal orders. Document everything. Mick could set us up to look bad and say we made errors." Dan looked sad. "I'm so sorry you were involved in this. I'll defend you all the way. The good old boys' club is strong in this hospital. They stick together."

The nurses were forced to interact with Mick over patient care issues. About 6 a.m., Dan and Liz were sitting at the desk getting caught up on charting when the door to Rocky's room opened. Buck pushed a wheelchair toward the ambulance entrance. He transported an unrecognizable patient swathed in blankets, head covered. Outside, Mick helped drag Rocky's limp form into the back of Buck's SUV.

At the end of the shift, CEO Connelly took the entire night shift aside, giving them a stern lecture on HIPAA regulations and patients' right to privacy. "We must all protect our patients. Dr. Rocky Manchester is on medical leave. His friends will see that he gets proper treatment, so he can return to his position here when the time is right."

Liz said, "Dan, I can't find his chart. I need to finish charting on Rocky's medical record, including the last dose of Romazicon I gave."

Dan scanned the desk and the treatment room. "The chart is gone. All the strips and ECG are missing. I think Buck took them."

When Liz asked Mick about the charting, he said, "Forget it. Buck took care of it."

* * *

Dan took Liz to a back corner in the cafeteria where they could eat, have coffee, and write notes about their disastrous night. They talked about the important details. Liz made a personal record of her recollections of Rocky's vital signs, ECG interpretations, and the medications she had given. Dan recommended she keep it in her possession since there was no formal medical record to be found.

After 8 a.m., Dan contacted his superior, to discuss the situation. She accompanied them to Human Resources and called CEO Connelly to join them. He pompously opened the meeting by reminding them of HIPAA regulations and asked about the new RN.

Liz spoke up, introduced herself and confronted him. "We have no intention of stating any patient name. This time it's much bigger than a patient privacy issue. Dan and I have been threatened with our jobs. We were harassed, and a gag order placed on us. We know our rights and are considering obtaining a lawyer."

Both administrators stiffened, jaws clenched.

Dan stated, "The ER is now an unsafe workplace, and we face retribution. Liz and I will levy formal charges and need your support."

"Let me get this straight." Sweat appeared across the CEO's furrowed brow. "You are placing charges against Buck Sabo and Mick Fuller? They are my two best ER physicians."

Liz stood up to emphasize her point. "We witnessed clear ethics violations. You have physicians treating a critical patient, using the facility, the equipment, medications, and personnel to care for a critical patient without paying the fees.

Then, Dr. Sabo stole the medical record and abducted the patient. That will not look good in the news."

"Hold on. Hold on. Hold on, Liz. I'll see this is rectified. You know the doctors were in turmoil with their cohort near death. They probably felt responsible for not helping him before this happened."

Dan shook his head. "That may be, but we're caught in the middle. We were verbally and physically threatened. I plan to charge Buck with assault. He threw me against the wall."

Walt leaned back and scoffed. "I can't believe he would do that."

Liz supported Dan. "I was there. I saw it. To clarify this, Mick had us trapped in a small room, his back against the door, blocking us from leaving. He said, 'Do not tell anyone about this. If the word gets out, I'll know it was you and there'll be hell to pay.'"

Dan agreed. "Exactly. Mick also said, 'I'll have your jobs.' We're here to document this incident and defend ourselves in public if we have to."

Sharon sat in silence, thinking about Liz and the stress the young nurse had endured since setting foot in Anchorage, after her first assignment to a bush community for an emergency and now this. She hoped Liz wouldn't leave town.

Walt wiped perspiration from his face. He placed his elbows on the table, fingers tented beneath his chin. "I see. This is a serious infraction in many ways. I recommend you lodge written harassment complaints against the two doctors through HR. Do not reveal the patient's name. I'll contact our legal department for advice on how to move forward."

Dan's boss appeared unstressed. "Dan, you're my strongest nurse leader and have my support. Liz, I'm sorry we met this way. Welcome to our staff. I will do my best to help both of you through this."

After documenting their experiences and completing the list of charges, Dan told her he'd find another nurse to cover the next shift.

Liz called a cab to take her to the motel. It was 9:30 a.m. by the time she'd finished eating the free breakfast Days Inn provided. She had just reached her room when Paul called. She told him about her night without exposing patient information. She didn't have to, he blurted out, "Rodney Manchester, the philandering SOB. I know Rocky. What are those guys doing jeopardizing their medical licenses for him?"

Liz sat on the bed. "It places the medical facility at risk, along with their medical licenses and our nursing licenses."

"I wish you had come with me yesterday. I had a great day flying and doing my bush clinic. I hope you don't work in ER again."

"Dan's in a bad situation. He worked flight nursing in the military. Maybe he should look for a different job."

Paul sounded angry. "You have to think about yourself. He may not be able to protect you in the future."

She lay on the bed and closed her eyes. "I'm so wound up. I hope I can go to sleep. When is your next clinic?"

"I promised Walt Connelly I'd do some paperwork at the hospital this afternoon. I have another flight in a couple days."

"Remember my so-called gag order when you talk to Walt."

"It wasn't Walt who put the gag order on you, right?"

"True, but he did say not to discuss this until he clarifies what the hospital legal team wants them to do."

* * *

In late afternoon, the ring of her cell phone awakened Liz in a sleep fog. She answered to an unfamiliar male voice. "Keep your mouth shut about Rocky . . ." then, unintelligible conversation in the background, and the call ended. The caller's number remained on the phone.

Liz telephoned Paul about the caller.

He swore. "I'll come over to talk in a few minutes."

She dressed and within the hour, Paul appeared. "I'm so sorry that happened to you last night. Walt was no help. Damn him. I told him he'd have my resignation if Sabo and Fuller aren't taken off staff."

Liz closed the door and led him to two chairs at a small table where she'd placed her laptop. "Thanks for coming over. These have been a strange couple of days. Did a black cloud follow me to Alaska?"

"This is not your fault."

"I'd understand if you don't want to work with me." She showed him her phone. "Do you recognize this number?"

"Nope. Not one I know. Let's look it up on a reverse directory and see if we can find out who it is."

An internet search popped up with the name Lander Sabo. "I've never heard Buck Sabo's first name. It must be Lander. I'm calling Walt Connelly right now."

The CEO answered.

"Walt, Liz received a threatening call from Buck. I will not have her harassed. I'm on my way back to the hospital to talk with the chief of staff. Sabo and Fuller better be gone by the end of the day."

Her eyes popped open at that comment. After he hung up, she said, "Really?"

Paul stood to leave. "I'll be back."

He returned smiling when her hair was still a tangle of wet curls "Wow, do you look great. Good news. The bastards are off duty and off premises, charged with disruptive physician behavior and Sabo, with physical assault on a nurse. Both must go before the Physician Disciplinary Committee and the Executive Committee. Their behavior will be reported to the State Medical Board."

"What about Rocky?"

"Tomorrow, he's headed back to a chemical dependency unit in the lower forty-eight."

"Walt acted fast."

"He knew his butt would be in a sling if he didn't. He is very unhappy with me. But he acted appropriately." Paul sat down on the bed. "After a good night's sleep, would you be up for a flight to a bush clinic to deliver some meds, then visit my friends on the way back to Anchorage?"

"I'd like that. I'm sure not ready to return to the ER."

Over a casual dinner, Paul talked about plans for the next day. "In a small village like Chugalak, the health aide Clara communicates with telemedicine physicians at the Health Center here in Anchorage, but there are some things you just can't do remotely, like feel abdomens and listen to lungs. Telemedicine works great for skin lesions and psychiatry."

"What meds are you delivering?"

"Clara has a patient with shingles on his face that could spread to his eye without an antiviral agent and steroids. The meds could go out on the mail plane tomorrow, but since I was going to fly to Talkeetna anyway, I can stop on the way and deliver them. It's quicker."

In front of Days Inn, he gave her a crushing hug before seeing her to the entrance. With a wave, he was gone, leaving Liz wishing he would stay.

Chapter 7   Flight from Terror

Liz sat on the motel bed, exhausted by little sleep and swirling thoughts. Devastation at the loss of Jack and his lies on the burning desert seemed far away, replaced with soothing green terrain and an amazing man. She visualized Paul's face, hands, and blue eyes. Nothing like Jack's dark features. Liz recalled the sensual surge nearly overloading her circuits when Paul held her before driving off. Her fingers swept the soft leather of her duffel bag as she dragged out a jogging outfit for sleepwear. The bag, another reminder of Jack.

After a hot shower, feeling relaxed and warm, she flipped open her laptop to check emails, the first from her friend Annie in Red Bluff: *I've been trying to call you. Things are chaotic. Check your phone for my message. Call me no matter what time it is. I can't write the details. I'm glad you left.*

Liz's fingers trembled as she punched in her friend's number. The cell phone rang and rang, then went to voice mail. Before Liz had finished leaving her message, a call came in. "Annie? What's going on?"

"Sit down. You won't believe this. I went out in the morning when I got off shift and found my car—the one you sold me—trashed in the hospital parking lot."

"I'm so sorry. It was a great car for one hundred dollars. I thought the Subaru would last two hundred thousand miles. We never had trouble with vandals at the hospital."

"Not vandals. Nothing as simple as that." Annie talked faster. "I called the police. I expected the BIA since we're on reservation land. The feds showed up. They confiscated my car."

"What are you talking about?"

"The feds, DEA, and ICE with immigration. They all interrogated me and other flight members. They're trying to connect us with Jack Sullivan."

"You aren't making sense."

"Jack ran drugs when he wasn't working here. Can you believe that? We've been flying with a Mexican drug runner."

"It can't be true."

"Jack lived two lives, maybe three. That's not all. The feds said they monitored calls he made to you. You wicked little girl. You believed in a psychopath. I had to hear it from them that you were sleeping with him!"

I sat on the bed, shocked. "I wanted to tell you, but he convinced me it was a bad idea to let people at work know about our relationship. Now, I know why."

"You're in danger. Drug runners are looking for you. Drug Enforcement and the FBI will be contacting you. They believe Jack stashed money and contact names with you. Were you planning to run away together?"

"No way, Annie. This is too weird and frightening. I was in love with Jack and so damn naïve I believed him. I had no idea he was married, and I sure as hell didn't know he was running drugs."

"None of us did. The NTSB is re-examining the helicopter wreckage. The DEA guy told me they suspect Jack's drug-running associates sabotaged the helicopter to kill him. You know, loosened screws or partially sawed through something to make it crash to take Jack down. They don't like being double-crossed and didn't care who they killed with him."

"They mean business." Liz paced. "Scary. I don't like being double-crossed either. That son of a bitch. What about his poor wife?"

"No one here knows where she lives. Based on what I understand right now, he took a lot of money, and the drug runners want it back. Everyone is trying to follow his trail."

Liz went over and checked the lock on her door. "He lived a life of lies. Had a wife and baby. Worked with us a week each month, and in his spare time flew drugs into the U.S. A busy man."

Annie continued, "DEA says he flew fixed wings under the radar, landing in rural Arizona, offloading the drugs and big money, but helping himself to more than his share."

Liz spewed, "I can't help the feds. I know nothing."

Annie sounded scared. "The feds want names they believe he stored on his computer and the drug dealers don't want the contact information of their operatives exposed. They also want their money. They all apparently believe you have both."

"Jack never said a thing to me." Liz hesitated, "Did you tell the investigators where I am?"

"No, they told me. They've monitored all your calls. The new cell phone Jack gave you has GPS tracking, but even without GPS, it's easy to identify the cell towers where calls originate."

Liz seethed, "Bastard. He stalked me electronically."

"Jack had you in his sights all the time, girl. You were duped by a charming liar."

Fear flooded Liz. Alone in a motel without protection, she rushed to the door and checked the lock again. "Do the drug dealers know I'm here? Will the feds protect me?"

"I hear some fast breathing. You should be scared, very scared. They killed Jack and our friends."

"What do I do? Run and hide or call the police? Will they believe me?"

"Now I understand why you passed out on the tarmac during the memorial service when I pointed out Jack's wife. What a shock! First his fiery death and then to find out the lying son of a bitch had a wife and baby. You aren't pregnant, are you?"

"No. I don't have that to worry about, but I don't know what to do."

"Trade in the damn cell phone and change your number. Tell your mom and dad what happened so they don't keel over when someone shows up on their doorstep."

Liz felt paralyzed at the thought. "Could they be in danger from the drug dealers? I need to call them."

"First call the DEA here in Arizona."

"Why don't they just call me?"

"They've been watching you, probably hoping you'd lead them to the money. The guys who came here sounded surprised you suddenly showed up in Washington State."

"So, were they watching me at my parent's home?"

"I'm sure they were. They also told me today you were in Anchorage. I didn't tell them you'd emailed me from Anchorage. They already knew. They seemed to know everything except where Jack stashed the cash."

Liz agreed to call Annie back when she had a new phone, then, collapsed on her bed. Stupid. Naive. She'd believed a philandering drug runner. She was being electronically stalked by killers. What had she done to herself?

Liz dialed the Arizona DEA number Annie gave her.

A harsh male voice answered.

Liz identified herself and stated her reason for calling.

"We were hoping you'd call in. Our agent just arrived in Anchorage. We have many questions for you, Ms. Elliot."

"My friend Ann just told me you thought I might be involved with this drug stuff. I'm not. I have no information. Jack Sullivan and I had a relationship for about three months. He lied. I certainly didn't know he was married."

The agent cleared his throat, trying to interrupt. "An agent will contact you tomorrow for an interview."

"I won't be available. I'm starting a job early in the morning. Send him over right now."

"You . . ."

Liz interrupted the agent. "I'm a victim, not a criminal. I'm a nurse. The job is very important to me. I don't want my employer to know about your investigation. This kind of accusation could ruin my career."

"I'll see what I can do. I'll have DEA Agent Russell call you in a few minutes."

* * *

An hour later, Liz awakened with a start when her phone rang. She heard a harsh, Latino-accented voice. "We want the money and the names."

"I don't know what you're talking about."

"Don't play dumb. Jack was your lover. Give us what we want, and we won't hurt you or your parents."

Liz went numb.

"We know where your parents live. Call me at the number on your phone when you're ready to talk. Don't do nothin' foolish. We're watchin' you."

The phone went silent.

Liz sat on the bed, exhausted, thinking, worrying about the future. Within moments, a loud knock on the door sent a jolt of adrenaline through her body. She held her breath, listening. The knock repeated, louder.

Liz tiptoed to the door and looked through the peephole into the hallway. She called out, "What do you want?"

Two men stood back from the door, official, wearing plain clothes, one held a badge in her view. "FBI. We need to talk to you." The taller, younger man holding the badge said, "I'm DEA Agent Russell out of Arizona here to talk to you with Special Agent Forbes, Anchorage FBI."

Liz's cell phone rang. She walked over to pick it up from the bedside table and answered.

"This is DEA Agent Franz in Arizona. I talked to you about an hour ago. Agent Russell will be showing up at your hotel to talk. He's bringing an Anchorage FBI agent with him."

"There are two men at my door right now. I'm afraid to open it. A Spanish-sounding man just called and threatened me and my parents. Please don't let them hurt my parents."

"Be assured, Ms. Elliot, your parents are under twenty-four-hour surveillance. They're safe."

Liz walked to the door. "Agent Franz, the men at my door say they are Forbes and Russell, but why should I believe what you say?"

"It's our men. Check their IDs."

Liz kept Franz on the line and opened the door, feeling like she was opening her door to wolves. She handed her phone to DEA Agent Russell. "Here, Agent Franz wants to talk to you."

Russell took the phone.

The other man closed the door and stood with his back to the wall. "Hello, Liz. You look just like your photo. I'm Anchorage FBI Special Agent Forbes. Sorry we've interrupted your evening."

Liz plopped onto her bed. "Please don't let them hurt my parents. They're simple, wonderful people who don't even own a gun."

Russell ended the call and pulled a chair up in front of Liz. He removed a laptop computer from his black shoulder bag, ready to input her answers. "Let's get started."

Questioning stretched on for two hours. Liz learned they'd been trying to follow her since her arrival in Anchorage. Forbes said sheepishly, "You slipped us for most of one day. Alaska doesn't have enough cell phone towers for accurate GPS tracking."

Liz pointed at the cell phone in Agent Russell's hand. "Obviously, the drug dealers have been tracking me. They called me tonight. The man said to call the number on the phone when I was ready to talk. They already killed Jack and two of my friends. I don't want to die. I'd give names and money if I had them."

Russell explained. "Lives mean nothing to them. We think Jack knew they were onto him and may have used you."

"Whenever he was in Red Bluff, Jack used my car. I suppose he could have left things hidden inside."

"We found nothing in the car to tie you to him or to drugs." Russell asked, "Did he give you anything?"

"The leather bag on the floor by my bed. He insisted I needed a new cell phone. I've only had it a month. I don't know even how to use most of the fancy features."

Russell checked the phone for recent calls. "We have a search warrant for this cell phone. I'll keep it." He pulled another phone from his pocket and handed it to Liz. "For now, take this replacement."

Forbes hoisted her duffel bag onto the foot of the bed. "We need to empty your bag."

Russell unzipped it. "I'll lay everything out on the bed. We can't let you do it. For all we know, you have a weapon."

Liz shook her head in disgust. "I've never owned a gun and wouldn't know how to use one."

Russell scanned the room. "Do you have anything else from Jack?"

"There is another piece of luggage, and a small Mexican painting I left at my parents' home."

Forbes removed a small black box the size of a cigarette pack from his pocket. As soon as he flipped a switch and waved the instrument over the outside of Liz's leather bag, it emitted a high-frequency sound. "The bag is bugged, Liz. Jack probably put a tracker in it so he could keep tabs on you. I wonder what else we'll find." He used a small digital camera to photograph the bag's contents as Russell spread her personal clothing on the bed.

Liz sat in a chair against the wall, infuriated. "It's embarrassing having my underwear and lacy bras laid out in front of perfect strangers."

"You're no stranger to us." Russell laughed. "We know you more intimately than you'd want to hear."

"What do you mean?" She glared. "How long have you been watching me?"

Russell flashed a lecherous grin. "Since you met Jack."

Bastards.

Forbes's scanner generated the same high-frequency tone over the empty bag. "Bingo! There is something hidden in the lining."

In one end, within a stitched pocket, they found an electronic bug and a one-inch stack of hundred-dollar bills. In the other end, they found a similar pocket with more money, along with a flash drive.

Russell grabbed the flash drive, before Forbes could say anything, he slid it into his computer, saved the contents, and opened a file.

At a glance, Liz saw photos and names.

Forbes growled, "Russell, you shouldn't have touched that drive. It might have important prints on it."

Russell shrugged off Forbes's comment. "I couldn't control myself." He smirked. "This ties Liz directly to the drug dealers."

Shocked by his statement, and furious, Liz said, "That's ridiculous! Jack used me."

The agents looked at each other as if trying to decide whether they could believe her.

"I'm already a sitting duck with all this electronic tracking stuff. The drug dealers will come to me. Can I help you catch them?"

Russell looked at his associate. "We'll have to discuss this further, but my thought is, leave the bug, the money, and the flash drive right here. Let them come."

Forbes pulled out his phone. "Too risky. Give me a minute to see what kind of backup I can generate." He faced away from them and made a call. After a short conversation,

Forbes turned back. "We'll have two men in the next room in thirty minutes. It will give us time to develop a plan. In the meantime, let's secure the evidence."

Russell offered Liz her confiscated phone. "Do you want to save some numbers from your old phone before I take it? Our numbers are programmed in your new phone, so you can call us.

Liz input her essential numbers and handed the phone back.

"We can track you on the new phone as long as you're in cell range, but remember, others can, too."

Forbes said, "Liz, we'll leave as soon as my men show up. You can take a change of clothes off the bed for tomorrow. The rest remains with the bag as evidence. Do you have any way to protect yourself?"

Liz decided she liked Forbes a lot better than she liked the DEA agent. "No."

Forbes appeared concerned, "Here, take this pepper spray and keep it on you. I hope you won't need it."

It was midnight by the time the men left.

Liz lay on the bed staring at the dark ceiling, listening to street noises and building creaks, until nightmares took over. Running. Hiding. She awakened after 8 a.m., tired and sweaty, feeling as though she hadn't slept at all. Suddenly, she remembered Paul would be picking her up.

Should she tell him? How could he trust her?

Liz dressed in boots, jeans, a red turtleneck, and a yellow hooded jacket. The only outfit she saved. Whenever she was blue or worried, she felt better wearing bright colors. She thought of her grandmother, who often told her to put on a little lipstick and she'd be fine.

On her way to the elevator, Liz dug deep in her small backpack, really a purse, her favorite gift from Jack she forgot to tell them about. She found a tube of lipstick and touched the light red to her lips. She never wore much makeup—she didn't need to. With her flawless tan skin, long dark lashes, and curly short hair, she looked great despite her bad night and was ready for whatever the day had in store. Liz fingered the small canister of pepper spray in her pocket as she stepped from the elevator and peered around the lobby, not sure what to look for.

Surveillance agents? Someone who might be a Mexican drug dealer?

What would they look like? Jack hadn't looked like a drug dealer.

Liz remained inside the lobby. When Paul arrived, she ran out and jumped in the Jeep. They chose breakfast from a buffet line at the hospital and then sat in a corner of the doctors' lounge, eating and talking. "Soon we'll be off on another adventure, Liz. The weather is great for flying."

"It should be fun." And, Liz thought, it will get me out of town to a safe location. She took her last bite of a bagel. "Thanks for breakfast."

Paul filled disposable cups with coffee for the road and handed one to Liz. This time, they walked to the garage stairway instead of running like they did when they were headed out to deliver Sal's baby. "I'll tell you more about telemedicine. It's become a useful tool for remote sites. Some villages have no outside communication except for a satellite phone in their health clinic."

"I can't imagine living in such isolation."

Paul navigated the sparse traffic and filled her in on aspects of the job he hoped she'd take. "Wintertime is the worst. With so little daylight to run solar panels, sometimes they run out of battery power. They use some gasoline generators, but the only personal contact they have from outside the village is when a plane on skis arrives with supplies."

Liz asked, "Do you fly on skis?"

"Wheel-skis. I can land on both snow-covered runways in the bush and pavement at Merrill Field. The villages keep the airstrips plowed when they can. I usually land on wheels but have the option to lower the skis and use them if necessary."

"Winter really complicates things."

"It does, both the unpredictable weather and the short hours of daylight."

"So, the health aide treats everything except when you show up?"

"She has to. There's no one else. They're good with kids, ear problems, and minor illnesses. Like Florry at Chugalak, Clare knows how to do pelvic exams and treat the sexually transmitted diseases that run rampant in the villages. Her care is protocol driven, with guidelines for common problems."

They parked near the hospital plane. Paul removed the tie-down ropes. Liz opened the cowling to check the oil. After checking out the Maule, they were airborne across the expanse of sea west of Anchorage. Liz looked down on the water, feeling uneasy. "That's a lot of water down there. What if the engine quits?"

"I always fly high enough to glide to the shore. You wouldn't last long in the frigid water, even if you survived impact. Your chances would be much better on the tidal flats if you are close enough to reach the shore—that is, if the incoming tide doesn't get you first."

She laughed at his dark humor "Great. Now, I really feel safe.".

"I carry survival gear the year round to be ready if I have an emergency landing. I even carry a weapon in the back, along with food and two sleeping bags."

"I thought summers were warm."

"Alaskan summer nights can be cold, just like on the desert. I carry a down jacket in my car, too. I've worn it on the fourth of July."

"I don't even own a warm jacket. This is a big change from desert survival gear. When I drove out on desert roads exploring, I carried water and a reflective blanket. Not much else."

"What were you looking for?"

"I liked visiting old mining towns and searched for fossils."

"Did you find anything interesting?"

"Rocks, with beautiful oak leaf fossils, and a few with tiny fish. I brought them home and left them with my parents. I love to learn about the past, about nature." Liz thought for a moment. "It's the future that scares me."

Paul glanced at her, thinking how beautiful she looked gazing over the Alaskan terrain, dark fluffy hair compressed on the sides by the headset. "Why the frown? Is it my flying?"

When she looked at him, he saw tears.

She quickly wiped one that trailed down her cheek. "It isn't you. I love it up here. I feel totally safe. It's on the ground that I'm afraid."

"Why?"

"Last night I got some bad news. I'm still in shock."

"What? What happened?"

"It's so bizarre, I considered not telling you."

"Are you sure you should have come with me today?"

"Very sure."

Liz shared the details, trying to be matter of fact, including her relationship with Jack, the helicopter crash, her reasons for leaving Red Bluff, and what the feds had found in her luggage. "I offered to act as a decoy to help them catch the drug dealers."

Paul tensed, pulling the plane into a turn as he stared at her. "They let you do that? Set you up on a drug deal?" Paul raised his voice in disbelief. "That's crazy. Refuse."

"It seemed like a good idea. The feds have had me under surveillance for weeks. They were even watching me when I was with my parents in rural Washington."

"You can't trust them just because they said they're federal agents. You need a lawyer."

"I trust them. Two FBI agents arrived to guard me before the others left my hotel room last night."

"I don't like this. It's too dangerous. You should stay out in the village where we're headed. No one will find you."

Paul leveled the wings and got back on course. His brow furrowed as he eased back on the throttle, starting their descent to the village.

The engine noise dropped.

Liz sat forward and scanned the instruments, wondering if something was wrong.

"Don't worry. We're descending. The village is straight ahead along the river."

Liz looked over the desolate land. "Alaska is huge, most of it uninhabited. It would be easy to hide here."

Paul sounded matter of fact. "That's why it's attractive to misfits and people trying to escape the law."

"I'm beginning to like Alaska for a lot of reasons. I could just disappear."

"There are big drug problems in Anchorage and in bush communities. I'll ask around for a reputable lawyer for you." He hesitated. "We could have trouble finding one. Last year, they arrested a prosecuting attorney for cocaine distribution. He took down a few friends with him, including a judge."

"It's amazing what people will do for money. The drug dealers in Arizona killed innocent medical personnel just to take out Jack. No telling what they'd do to get what I might have, but I could end up with a crooked lawyer who is on their side. That's not reassuring."

"Maybe the agents are in on it. They have a lot of temptations. Taking money would be easy. Who would know?"

"Now, I'm really creeped-out after having them in my hotel room, but I think they're for real. The DEA guy, Russell, came up here from Red Bluff, and FBI Special Agent Forbes, is local. They showed me their IDs."

"There are crooks in every profession, but my biggest concern is the dealers. Your life is at risk if it turns out you could identify them."

"I didn't tell you I received a call from a guy with a Spanish accent last night."

Paul grimaced. "More bad news."

"He called just before the agents arrived unannounced. The agent I talked to in Red Bluff said Agent Russell was arriving in Anchorage and wanted to talk to me today. I refused."

"I bet they loved that."

"They tried to force the issue, but I said I wanted to talk to Russell immediately and clear my name. Instead of calling me, two guys just showed up at my door."

"They probably wanted to surprise you, thinking you'd try to run."

"I suppose. The DEA guy confiscated my cell phone and gave me a replacement. Said they had a warrant but didn't show it to me."

Paul keyed the radio and announced their arrival at the isolated airport. "Look down. You can see the windsock and a wind triangle. The triangle rotates like a weather vane and points into the wind, showing the direction to land. The wind sock tail points away from the wind."

"I see them, but the wind sock looks very small. So do the houses, they look like Navajo huts."

Paul circled, preparing to land on the small gravel strip. "It gets very cold. Small is good when you're trying to stay warm."

The plane lined up with the strip and lost altitude as Paul decreased power. "You always want to land and take off into the wind. It provides more lift. When landing, the wind will keep the plane flying until you reduce power to the point of stalling just before touchdown. In other words, think about it as if you're flying out of the large end of the wind sock into the wind."

Liz reviewed the concept in her mind, thinking she might need the information later.

They touched down, slowed to a stop, and then back-taxied to the end of the runway. "The wind usually blows this direction out here. We'll likely be taking off in the same direction we landed. If we park here, we're set up for departure."

Liz thought about her predicament. "I felt safe up there, safe talking to you. With all this stuff about being bugged, I can't even call my parents. The feds said they have my parents' home staked out and will tell them I'm safe."

"You're safe here, except for the mosquitoes." When the propeller stopped, a gray cloud of buzzing insects blanketed the plane. Paul opened his door to exit, allowing dozens of fliers with their high-pitched hum to enter the cockpit. "I didn't tell you how dense mosquitoes are in bush country. Out in the wind, mosquitoes dissipate. The homes are primitive, but they have screens. Inside, we'll be fine."

"Why are the mosquitoes so much worse here?"

"Inland, across the tundra, there is more standing water, perfect for mosquito breeding." Paul swatted mosquitoes. "Let's run to the clinic."

Liz looked around. "How do villagers get food up here?"

"Bulk grocery orders arrive by air about every two weeks. Most residents are subsistence living. Fishing and hunting the year round."

"I can see why Tim ran off. This is culture shock for someone from LA. At least in the desert, there are roads and a few stores. Not many bugs."

The health aide walked out to meet them. Paul handed her the medications. Clare greeted Liz and apologized for the swarming insects.

Paul and Liz ran back to the Maule and climbed in. They spent the next few minutes killing pests that boarded with them.

"We are about half an hour from Talkeetna where my friends George and Betsy live. Flying home, we'll follow the Parks Highway for about ninety miles south to Anchorage."

Liz noted miles of flat land cut by winding rivers. In the distance, a narrow highway emerged from the trees, covered by a ribbon of moving cars and motor homes.

Paul said, "Talkeetna is a staging area for Denali mountain climbers. Pilots fly them to the Ruth Glacier base camp."

"Crazy. They land on a glacier?"

"It is rough, icy terrain. We could fly over the area for a look sometime, but I wouldn't land there. I'm too much of an amateur." Paul pointed. There's the strip. I'll circle to check wind direction and be sure it's clear of animals."

Liz looked down. "What animals? We didn't have to worry about big creatures on the desert."

Paul scanned the sky and announced their approach. "I've seen deer and moose on the runway. When we're landing, hang onto the yoke gently. Pay attention to my feet and hands. Landing is easy."

Liz nodded. Concentrating on flying provided distraction from other disturbing thoughts.

They circled, descended, and lined up with a narrow, paved runway appearing no wider than a sidewalk. As they lost altitude, the runway emerged as a substantial paved strip.

Paul stopped near the south end of the runway. He killed the engine, popped open his door, and got out.

Liz opened her door. Paul swung her to the grass. His hands around her waist infused a feeling of strength and safety.

He pointed at a little house near the runway." Betsy always has coffee on."

Paul slid ropes through ring attachments beneath both the wings and on the tail, typing them to ground chains provided at the parking place. "There isn't much wind now, but it can come up suddenly, so I always tie my planes down."

The couple walked through a gate in the perimeter fence and headed toward the house. Two gangly gray dogs barked joyously and wagged bushy tails as Paul and Liz approached. A face appeared at the door, "George!" Paul called and waved. "Hi. I'm glad we found you home. I have someone I want you to meet."

Before they reached the door and exchanged greetings with George, Liz smelled coffee and fresh bread. Paul introduced her.

George called back inside to his wife, "Betsy, we have company. Paul is here with Liz, a new nurse."

A miniature lady in black tights and a large red sweatshirt appeared in the doorway. Fluffy white hair puffed into a cotton ball framed her deeply wrinkled face. "Hi, you two. How'd you pick up such a good-lookin' lady, Paul?"

"I told her we were coming here to have coffee. I didn't know you were baking." He turned to Liz. "Betsy's the best cook in Alaska."

"Don't listen to him. I spent the first half of my life dealing blackjack in Vegas, and the second half I spent learning how to cook for George and our dogs." Her gravelly laugh sounded like a cigarette cough.

The dogs followed them inside.

George said to the tallest dog, "Bo, show Liz where your candy is. Maybe she'll give you a piece."

Bo walked over to Liz. His intense golden eyes captured hers. He herded her to a kitchen cabinet and sat down. He kept Liz's gaze and, with his nose, pointed at a drawer and pawed the knob.

"Does Bo understand everything you say?" she said in amazement.

"Pretty much. They both do, but Bo's an alpha male and was harder to train."

Liz asked, "Bo, do you want some candy?"

His tail swept the floor and swished his furry partner sitting beside him. Echo's eyes fixated on the drawer.

George said, "I guess Echo wants some, too. She follows Bo everywhere."

Golden eyes watched as Liz opened the drawer. A little afraid they might snap the candy out of her hand, she removed one piece of butterscotch and cautiously peeled off the wrapper.

"Bo, let Echo have hers first." Bo lay on the floor at George's voice.

Echo gently took the candy from Liz.

Then Bo sat and watched as Liz unwrapped his piece. His lips barely grazed Liz's fingers.

"These dogs are amazing. Real dogs, not brainless mops like my mother used to have."

"They're rescue wolf mixes found chained to trees without shelter, starving. The breed has a reputation for being unpredictable. We agreed to take them, knowing we needed to gain absolute control."

"We've spent the past year training them." Betsy patted Echo's head. "We trust them with our lives."

Paul petted both dogs. "It's isolated here in winter. The dogs provide protection for Betsy when George is away."

A transmission from a radio perched on a shelf near the door shot a jolt of adrenaline through Liz's body. She jumped up to listen. George increased the volume.

"Break, break. KF7TLT."

George answered, "KF7TLT, this is AL7AU, go ahead."

"Emergency call, George. State Trooper 76 at Mile 95 on the Parks Highway requests assistance at a moose-versus-car injury accident. Is Doc Leonard in town?"

George asked Paul, "Can you go? It's about five miles. We could be there in a few minutes."

Paul looked at Liz. She nodded.

"AL7AU, Betsy and I have a doc and nurse visiting us. Tell the trooper we'll be there in about ten minutes."

Chapter 8   Life Flight

Paul ran for the airplane to get a jump kit of medical supplies. Liz ran after him. "Do you have major trauma supplies, lines, needles, airways?"

"They're in the small pack." He grabbed a pack and a slotted, rolled backboard from the baggage area.

Liz took them and set off for the open Jeep.

Paul shouldered a large pack and joined George and Liz. He handed Liz a pair of protective gloves and stuffed a pair into George's shirt pocket.

"Thanks. I hope I don't need them." George talked as they bounced over a dirt road. "Betsy said she'd call old Doc Leonard and see if he is available to help. He seldom does trauma work anymore. Hard of hearing and crippled up now."

Traffic blocked the highway and impeded George's passage until he moved to the shoulder to bypass the line of stopped vehicles. The five miles seemed to take forever, but it gave Liz time to paw through the medical packs to see what Paul carried.

Paul looked back at Liz rummaging through his kits. "I hope I have what we need."

"It looks good. What happened to our scenic flight, Doc?" Liz smiled. Her heart beat fast in anticipation of what they'd find.

"In Alaska, you never know what you'll run across," George said. "I'm just glad we aren't going to a bear mauling. I've had my fill of those."

Liz commented, "Based on the size of the bear mount at the airport, I don't see how anyone could survive a mauling."

An SUV, sitting sideways on the highway, had hit a large, sleek animal. The deceased moose with huge antlers lay awkwardly embedded in the left front of the vehicle. Blood streamed from the animal, forming a coagulated mass mixed with leaking radiator fluid.

Carrying the jump kit, Liz was out of the Jeep running toward the vehicle before the guys even put their feet on the ground. Paul followed her, bringing the short backboard and large pack.

Liz scanned the area in automatic triage mode. Windshield shattered by the moose impact. Crying toddler restrained in a backseat chair. Seat-belted driver hanging forward over his shoulder restraint, breathing, blood covering his face. A crying woman standing outside the vehicle. "Paul, the steering wheel is bent. He took quite an impact. Respirations fast. One eye swelled shut. There's a lot of blood running from his forehead lac."

Paul jerked on the driver's door handle but was unable to open the jammed door. "We'll have to extricate him through the passenger side. The kid looks okay."

"I love it when the kids are crying. At least you know they have an open airway." Liz talked to the woman and had her sit in the trooper's car, and then she climbed into the back seat of the crashed vehicle to perform a quick survey on the child. She spoke gently to the crying little boy, palpating his head, neck, chest, and belly as she talked. After releasing the seat belt restraining the child seat, Liz dragged him out the door, seat and all.

Paul entered the car through the passenger side to work on the driver.

George arrived, panting. "The trooper called for help. Another trooper relayed his request to dispatch the Lifeguard medical helicopter out of Regional Hospital in Anchorage." He took a few deep breaths. "The estimated flight time is about an hour. I'll do crowd control and help move vehicles past the wreck unless you need me for something else."

Liz handed the crying toddler to George. "I think he's okay, just scared." Liz pulled a dirty pink rabbit from the car and snuggled the toy against the child's chest.

A trooper tried to calm the anxious young woman seated in the back of his car.

George placed the rabbit-hugging toddler next to his mom. The boy settled down, sucking his thumb, when he realized his mother was sitting beside him.

Liz examined the woman and gave her a gauze pad to hold over her bleeding forehead laceration.

"Is Ken dead? Oh, please, tell me he's okay. He wasn't moving."

"Ken has a head injury. Dr. Lasher is with him and a medical helicopter is on the way. I'm Liz. I'm a nurse. Does Ken have any allergies? Is he diabetic?"

"No. He's healthy, doesn't even take aspirin."

Liz said, "You take care of your little boy and wait here in the trooper's car. We'll let you know how Ken is doing after we get him out of the car."

The trooper squatted by the open door, looking at the woman and child. "I'll keep her here with the little boy. George is directing traffic."

Liz ran to help Paul.

George moved observers away from the SUV, away from the injured man.

Paul was kneeling on the front passenger seat, awkwardly supporting Ken's neck to open the unconscious man's airway. Liz entered the back seat with the short board and slipped it behind Ken's back with Paul's help. Liz reached over the seat and took control of Ken's neck, holding it in alignment to reduce the risk of paralysis if he had an unstable neck fracture.

Paul rotated the unresponsive man, so he lay flat on the seat.

With help from bystanders, they dragged the injured man out, one on each leg and one on each side at his waistline, using his jeans as a sling to carry him. They placed him on the ground and stood back. "Good job. Thanks for the help," Paul said, and he looked up into the calm face of his skilled companion.

Liz knelt, stripped open Ken's shirt, with trauma shears from Paul's pack, sliced his jeans from the pant bottoms through the waist band. That allowed them to see his limbs and examine his body without clothing obstructing their view. The trooper and George dispersed the onlookers and kept them cordoned away from Paul and Liz.

Paul caught Liz's eyes. "You're amazing. I've never seen a woman undress a man so fast."

Liz locked on his clear blue eyes, wondering if he was trying to make light of the situation to defuse some of their stress. Keeping a neutral expression and without the slightest hesitation, she raised an eyebrow, "Paul, I've had a lot of practice."

He flashed a smile.

They felt Ken's chest, looking for fractured ribs and observing his breathing. Liz's gloved hand touched Paul's. A distracting zing of emotion shot through her body. She saw his expression, wondering if he'd felt anything or it was just her imagination? Was it stress? Was the life-and-death situation charging her emotions?

Liz didn't have to wonder very long. Paul took her hand and squeezed it, generating a flow of energy to her heart. She said, "His chest is bruising. Feel this." Liz placed his hand beneath hers to feel the area, wishing she could place his hand somewhere else. She took a deep breath. "There's air in the tissue. Rib fractures and a pneumothorax. Do you have a stethoscope?"

"Nope. It's in another exam kit in the plane. Dang!"

Paul placed his ear close to Ken's chest. "I can hear breath sounds on both sides."

"Good, but he's working hard," Liz noted. "His belly feels soft. He's starting to move." She felt each vertebra in Ken's neck, checking for injury.

Paul helped Liz wrap a pressure dressing over a three-inch forehead laceration to slow the bleeding, Given Ken's awakening and confused state, they tried to keep him calm and prevent any movement that could aggravate injuries.

"I love this stuff." Liz pulled a roll of duct tape from one pack. "Never leave home without it."

"I agree. I keep a roll in my car and my Super Cub."

"What's a Super Cub?" Liz asked as she fastened the backboard straps across Ken's waist.

"It's one of those little airplanes on balloon tires that can land anywhere."

"You mean you have your own plane? Don't you get enough flying at work?"

"There aren't many roads in Alaska where you can drive to great fishing spots. You have to fly to get there."

Ken lurched, trying to get up.

Liz ordered, "Ken! Stop moving! You were in an accident. Lie down." She held his shoulders. "Your wife and baby are okay. You're going to a hospital for treatment."

Ken tried to talk, gurgling, spewing blood, ". . . can't breathe, can't breathe . . ."

"Paul, he's looking worse." She checked his pulse. "It's weak and fast." She leaned down and listened against Ken's chest. "Breath sounds are less on the right now. His trachea is off midline. Damn, he's developed a tension pneumothorax."

"Shit. Doesn't that mean we have to needle his chest?"

Liz nodded. "We have to decompress the right side to relieve the trapped air and allow the lung to expand."

Paul dug through the medical bag and came up with a chest tube kit with a large needle and a one-way Heimlich valve.

Liz ripped open the wrapper.

A huge bearded male dressed in dirty clothes rushed up, out of breath and sweating.

Liz looked up at him, focusing on an exquisitely tattooed snake coiled around his muscular forearm that disappeared beneath a sweat-stained undershirt sleeve with a pack of cigarettes rolled inside it. He touched her shoulder, saying, "I know CPR. I can help."

"He doesn't need CPR. He has a collapsed lung." Liz pushed his hand off her shoulder. "We don't need help."

The man grabbed the chest tube package out of Liz's hand. "Show me your doctor's license."

Squatting next to Ken, Paul stood up. "Hey, I'm a doctor, sir. Please stay back. We don't need your help."

The man pushed Paul backwards, flattening him on the ground. The man was on Paul, fist held back and ready to strike. George saw the commotion and stormed over, screaming, "Get the hell out of the way! Keep your hands off the doctor!"

Liz retrieved the chest tube package as Paul and George grappled with the man.

"A damn doctor killed my kid!" the man yelled. "You doctors don't know what the hell you're doing."

George yelled for more help. Bystanders took the unruly man to the ground and held him while a trooper applied handcuffs.

Shaken, Paul moved back into position to help Liz. He whispered, "Are you okay? I never thought I'd need this chest tube. I've never done one." He took a deep breath. "I've never even seen a tension pneumo. I hated ER."

She scrubbed Ken's chest with an iodine swab. "It's okay, I've done a few. They're easy. I love this work. Just count down three interspaces and advance the needle over the top edge of the lower rib, mid-clavicular line."

Liz counted down the ribs and pointed. "That's where it goes."

Paul's hands trembled as he laid the package within her reach.

Ken stopped moving. Liz shook his shoulder and felt his carotid artery. "I can barely feel a pulse. Ken, can you hear me?"

No response.

Liz slipped on sterile gloves and uncapped the large needle. Her small hands wearing gloves big enough to fit Paul's, she pushed the needle through the skin at the designated interspace.

Ken didn't flinch.

A whoosh of air told Liz the needle was deep enough. She advanced a tube attached to a special one-way valve through the large needle. Once it was in place, she withdrew the needle.

Paul handed her wide adhesive tape and helped secure the tube. "I prefer being the nurse. Glad you're here." Paul pressed on Ken's neck, checking his carotid artery pulse. After a few minutes, he said, "Ken's pulse is stronger. I'll try to start an IV line."

Ken remained still—very still.

Liz felt Ken's facial bones and inside his mouth. "He has an off-set lower jaw fracture. He'll be tough to tube with all the blood in his throat, but we need to intubate him. I didn't see a laryngoscope and tube. Do we have them?"

"They're in a kit tucked into the side of the large bag. I haven't done a tube in years."

"I placed one about four weeks ago in Arizona, a few in the past year."

"This one's yours. I'll get the equipment ready." Paul checked his watch and wiped perspiration from his face. "I hear the chopper."

Liz cleared blood from Ken's mouth and opened the intubation kit while Paul started the IV.

The sound of the helicopter got closer, and it landed on the highway. When the flight team materialized beside Liz and Paul, saline was running wide open and Liz had the laryngoscope in her hand. She looked up into the faces of the flight team and felt the relief she'd seen in the faces of so many ill-prepared rescuers she'd assisted in the past when her team flew to a scene call. "Glad you're here, guys. Thanks for coming."

Chapter 9 A Life Saved

Hi, team, I'm Paul Lasher, a Native Health Center doc. This is my friend Liz Elliot. She's a flight nurse." He described the patient's injuries and treatments, including the chest tube. "Had a tension pneumothorax until Liz decompressed his right chest. His carotid pulse improved after the tube."

The male flight nurse kneeled beside Ken, checking his heart and abdomen and listening to his lungs. "Great job, you two. You obviously saved his life. I hear breath sounds on both sides now."

"Another moose versus car, huh?" The other medic connected a second IV bag and squeezed in fluid. "The moose usually wins." He looked at the dead moose. "Was there anyone else in the car?"

Liz gestured toward a trooper car. "A wife and child. They're stable but should be transported and evaluated."

George heard Liz. "The troopers have a ground unit en route from Palmer. They're thirty minutes out. I'll go back to check on the cute little kid."

Liz interrupted. "We have to get Ken intubated. Comatose, head injured, and a pneumothorax. He can't maintain his airway and needs better oxygenation."

The flight nurse said, "The pilot is bringing our stretcher. Let's get him on it so I have a better view for tube placement."

Liz agreed. "It's much harder trying to do it lying on the ground."

The four medical practitioners quickly rolled Ken to his side and palpated and examined his back. They placed him on a padded long board and lifted him onto the transport stretcher.

The flight nurse spread equipment on Ken's chest.

Liz noted the tube with lighted stylet. "I'm glad you have good equipment. He may be a difficult tube placement with the facial fractures and blood in his airway."

The male nurse voiced confidence but hyperventilated as his shaky fingers opened Ken's mouth, pulling his unstable fractured jaw forward to take a look inside.

The flight nurse and medic worked well together, obviously veterans in the business. Ken bit down on the blade and tried to push the nurse's hand away as the nurse suctioned and looked again,

Liz grabbed Ken's arm, helping, but the flight team was now in charge. She and Paul were acting as Good Samaritans, not subject to malpractice suits when helping at a roadside emergency. Liz cringed as she watched the difficult process, feeling professional pressure to be sure Ken received proper treatment. She hoped they carried paralytic and sedative drugs. If Ken woke up, they'd never get a tube in without drugs.

Other thoughts ran through her mind as she scanned the crowd and recalled the violence of the man who was now handcuffed and in custody. In a crisis, some people run away and others try to be helpful, sometimes to everyone's detriment.

Liz recalled her worst experience with bystanders, which occurred when a doctor tried to take over a scene with a critical accident victim. It turned out the doctor was a psychiatrist who needed a shrink himself. He knew nothing about trauma.

Police carted him off in cuffs, too.

"We'll have to paralyze him." The nurse's statement brought her thoughts back to Ken.

"I agree," Liz said with relief.

The medic pulled out two vials and syringes.

"Give five milligrams of Versed, then one hundred and fifty milligrams of sux.

The medic pushed the two medications into the IV line.

Sedation, paralytics, oxygen, suction. Within seconds, Ken stopped breathing because of the paralytic. His muscles relaxed so they could easily place the tube. It had to be done rapidly because without respiratory effort, his lungs were receiving no oxygen. As time passed, his brain would suffer from the lack of oxygen.

Sweating and frustrated, the flight nurse repeatedly searched in Ken's bloody throat.

The patient received oxygen flow by mask between attempts to place the breathing tube, but because he was paralyzed and had blood accumulating in his airway, Ken's oxygen saturation was surely dropping. They were unable to adequately bag him with high-flow oxygen.

Liz cringed. Dammit. With so much blood in his throat, he'd arrest if they didn't get a tube in fast. "Could I try? I've done a lot of them."

The nurse handed her the lighted laryngoscope and tube. "Go for it."

First Liz pulled Ken's jaw forward and suctioned the throat with a crude battery-operated device. She took the laryngoscope. To the nurse, she said, "Please help by pulling up on his jaw like this. Give me a little pressure over his neck at the cricoid. Maybe it will help me see the cords."

She took a deep breath and, straining on her tiptoes to see, Liz inserted the blade of the scope and searched. "Give me more cric pressure." She pulled up on the scope. "Tube." Liz held out her hand, and the nurse placed the endotracheal tube in her hand. Liz slid it in. She let out her breath and exclaimed, "It's in. I saw it go through the cords."

Liz inflated the balloon around the tube to seal it against the inside of the trachea.

The medic squeezed the bag. Both sides of Ken's chest expanded.

"Wow! Liz, you're great. Do you need a job? We've got an opening."

She shook her head. "I'm taking a break from flight nursing."

"You'd never know it by lookin' at you." The medic beamed. "Great work for someone who's on vacation."

Their smiles ended quickly. They rushed Ken to the helicopter, where the pilot helped lift the loaded stretcher inside. The partners in navy blue jumpsuits climbed in and closed the door.

Liz and Paul stepped back, shielding their faces from the cloud of debris stirred up by the main rotor as it spooled up, slowly at first and then faster and faster.

The helicopter lifted off.

Paul stood silent, relieved. He looked down into Liz's face, wanting to be sure she heard him over the rising helicopter noise. "Great job, Liz." He repeated, "Great job."

They turned away from the dust cloud and walked toward the trooper's car. Paul said, "Let's find George and get out of here."

Liz touched his arm. "First let's tell Ken's wife about his injuries and where to find him."

They found George entertaining the giggling little boy. His mother sat in the back seat, one hand on the child and her eyes closed, her face streaked with tears.

Two troopers flagged a long line of cars, campers, and semis past the crashed vehicle and moose carcass. Paul opened the back door of the trooper's vehicle. Liz sat beside the distraught woman, who opened her eyes when she heard Liz's voice.

The woman gripped Liz's arm. "Please tell me Ken will be all right."

"He has serious injuries, with rib fractures and a collapsed lung, but he is doing much better. The flight team left with him. They're en route to Anchorage."

"What hospital? We're on vacation from Washington State. Our car is totaled, and I don't have a way to get to Anchorage."

The trooper said, "Ken is going to Regional, but you'll be going to the Palmer Hospital. An ambulance from Palmer will be here any minute."

"I don't need an ambulance," the woman said. "I just need a ride for me and the baby."

"Dr. Lasher and I recommend you go with the ambulance crew. They'll check your vital signs. You have a laceration on your face that needs stitches. You might need an X-ray. Your left ankle is swelling."

The woman tried to get out of the car and discovered she was unable to bear weight on her left foot. She sat back down, "I guess you're right, but it can't be broken. I already walked on it. I'll get checked out and then rent a car. I think I'll be able to drive." She looked at her smiling baby. "Gage is looking happy. I love him so much. Ken is a wonderful father. We'll get through this."

Paul's voice wavered. "Ken was doing much better after he had the breathing tube in. I think he'll make it."

Liz studied Paul's face as he talked to the wife. He appeared strained, and his eyes were moist.

Paul stroked the baby's hair. He took one of the boy's small hands. Delicate fingers curled around Paul's index finger and held on tight.

The trooper explained to the wife, "Your car will be towed to Palmer. Do you want to get your things out before we move it?"

The little boy still gripped Paul's hand.

"I'll bandage her head while you and George get the luggage. The ambulance can transport it with her."

Paul gently withdrew his finger from the boy's grip and tousled the child's hair. He stacked two suitcases on the shoulder of the highway. "I'm surprised the airbag didn't deploy. If it had gone off like it's supposed to, it might have prevented Ken's chest injury."

The trooper heard the comment. "I think his seat belt caught late. He's lucky to be alive after impacting the steering wheel hard enough to bend it. I've seen a lot of fatalities from moose collisions."

As the wail of an ambulance neared, the woman said, "Thank you all so much. I'm sorry, I didn't even tell you my name. I'm Wilda."

"Nice to meet you. Sorry about the accident. Do you have a cell phone so we can call you?"

Liz pulled out her cell phone and input the information.

Paul explained, "Out here, there are few cell towers. Closer to Anchorage, we'll have better coverage again. We'll call you later after we check on Ken."

Liz checked her new phone. "Here you are telling her there is no coverage and I've got two bars."

George looked over her shoulder. "It's not bad. They put in a new cell tower recently."

Exhilarated but tired after their ordeal, the three scrubbed off sweat and dust before sitting down at the table. "I made venison barley soup while you were gone." Betsy filled their bowls. "It's one of George's favorites. I thought you'd need more than a slice of bread and coffee before taking off for Anchorage."

Visiting with Betsy and the dogs provided emotional decompression for George, Paul, and Liz. They discussed the accident while eating.

Liz finished her large bowl of soup. "Delicious. Thanks so much. I really needed it." After lunch, she sat on the living room floor leaning against the couch. The dogs circled and lay beside her. She placed a hand on each dog.

Echo rested her head on Liz's lap. Liz felt Paul's hand on her shoulder. He gave her a little squeeze.

Liz looked up.

"Amazing job, Liz. If I stick with you, you'll turn me into a trauma doc."

"We did it together. It's good we were able to get there in time and had your equipment." Golden dog eyes focused on her face.

Liz admired George and his small wife relaxing in armchairs near a potbelly stove. She pictured them the same in winter with a roaring fire. "You have a great place. I love it here, and I love your dogs."

"You can stay here any time." Betsy gestured toward the back of the house. "We have two extra bedrooms. We can take a walk into town and show you how country folk live."

"To a foreigner who just left the Arizona desert, this is paradise."

"You aren't a foreigner anymore. Those dogs won't let anyone who isn't a member of their pack come within twenty feet." George sounded pleased. "They don't take to many people like they have to you."

Liz stroked Echo's smooth gray head and stared into her wild eyes.

The tip of her tail wagged. She looked at George. "Good girl, Echo. You take care of Liz."

Paul tapped Liz on the shoulder. "I think we better head back. I don't want to go, but, for a scenic flight, it's been a long day." He helped Liz to her feet after she carefully moved Echo's head from her lap.

"We'll all walk you out to the gate."

Paul and Liz did the plane walk-around, checking everything, including the fuel. He had to remove a stepstool from the baggage compartment to make it possible for Liz to check the fuel level in the wing tanks. After that, she opened an access door to check the oil, showing the stick to Paul before reinserting it and tightening the ring.

"You learn fast. Thanks."

The engine caught on the first try. After they were airborne and well above the trees, Paul circled back and rocked his wings, saying goodbye to the foursome on the ground.

They waved and wagged as the plane headed back to Anchorage.

It was after 5 p.m. by the time they landed in Anchorage. "Sharon will be gone by now. I know she'll want to talk to you tomorrow. Hopefully I haven't scared you away from taking the job."

"Today was pretty exciting. I still don't know exactly what the job entails."

"I can answer some of your questions after we land. It's easier to talk on the ground than through this intercom." Paul leveled out and eased back the power. "Do you feel up to going over to Regional Hospital to check on Ken?"

"Sure, I'll come with you. I'd like to see how he's doing, and then we can call his wife."

* * *

The ER doctor phoned Wilda from Ken's bedside, explaining his CT findings and the treatment he required. Ken remained sedated and, on a ventilator, recovering from the head injury, and would require surgery to stabilize his jaw.

Waking up, confused and with post-concussion symptoms, he fought the airway tube. They remained with him as he awaited the oral surgeon evaluation and stabilization of his broken mandible. He seemed to understand Wilda and Gage were okay.

They held the phone to his ear so Wilda could talk to Ken, even though he couldn't speak because of the airway tube. Ken relaxed after hearing her voice. An acquaintance of the Palmer doctor said he would drive her and Gage to Anchorage in the morning.

With Ken stable and the young family reconnected, Liz and Paul felt comfortable leaving. The exhausted duo walked out of Ken's ER room, anxious to find food.

A nurse stopped them. "Dr. Chrisman wants to talk to you." She motioned to a young man in blue scrubs and introduced them. "These are the two people our flight team said saved Ken's life."

"Good to meet you. Chuck Chrisman." They shook hands. "Ken is a lucky man." Dr. Chrisman directed his comments to Paul, who towered over Liz. "He never would have survived without your treatment."

"It wasn't me. Liz did the interventions. She's a flight nurse out of Arizona up here visiting. We happened to be close by when the accident call came in."

"Liz, you did everything right. I thank you. Ken will thank both of you when he's able." Dr. Chrisman added, "If you decide to stay in Alaska, Liz, we need a flight nurse."

"Thanks, but I'm not looking for a helicopter job. I'm here visiting. We were fortunate Paul had the gear we needed. He does village clinics with the Native Health Center. You know, flies into the remote villages. Today, we happened to be in Talkeetna visiting friends at the time of the accident."

"Do you mind if our PR person talks with you? I think the newspaper would be interested in doing a feature article. It's a terrific story."

"It's okay by me. How about you, Liz?"

"It's fine."

"Great. Suzie, would you call Admin and see if Nita is still here? They had a board meeting tonight, so our PR person may be in house."

Dr. Chrisman excused himself. "I have to get back to work. Thanks for agreeing to talk to a reporter. Our flight program could use some good publicity. The reason we have an opening for a flight nurse is because our chief nurse committed suicide after she was named in a bogus malpractice lawsuit."

Paul and Liz exchanged a glance. Liz said, "I'm so sorry."

"The patient died. It was not her fault, but the accusations devastated her. The case was dropped, but Holly is dead. It's been a huge blow to morale." Chrisman turned to leave and then added, "The flight team is superhuman, and they don't get the credit they deserve."

The nurse walked with Paul and Liz to a quiet room usually used to counsel bereaved family members. At the news of the suicide, Liz felt terrible, thinking about how doctors and nurses were not appreciated. They saw so much, did so much, and few people realized or cared.

Paul sensed her sadness and placed an arm around her shoulders. "Too bad someone couldn't help her in time." The nurse handed them each a cup of coffee.

Moments later, a flamboyant blonde with a camera pranced in and introduced herself as Nita. She snapped a few photos of them and then gathered the flight medic and nurse who had transported Ken for more photos. Outside on the helipad, in waning light, she snapped photos of the four of them near the helicopter.

"When Ken improves and can talk, I'll see if I can get some photos and call a reporter to interview him and his wife. I'll call the paper after we're done here. I'm sure they'll want to do a story. I need to have you sign a photo release for me."

They signed the papers and left.

Back in the Jeep, Paul said, "Are you good karma or bad?"

Liz shook her head. "Maybe the two of us are carrying black clouds over our heads. When I worked in the ER, some of the nurses accused me of being a magnet for trauma. Maybe there's some truth to that."

Paul sounded unconvinced. "Maybe, but things tend to work out for the best."

"Before we talk about anything else, food sounds good—anything."

"Since you have already tasted my cooking, how about trying an Italian place? Thirteen Coins is right downtown near the Captain Cook."

"Let's go."

* * *

Sitting in high-backed rotating bar chairs, oblivious to those nearby, they watched chefs prepare flaming dishes and flip stir-fry orders into the air, sending up surges of fire from oil splashes on gas burners. Sipping glasses of Cabernet, they conversed like old friends.

"I was thinking back over our day," Paul said. "I can't get the image of Ken's gurgling breath and shock state from my mind. He came so close to dying, leaving behind his wife and little boy."

Liz took a sip, savoring the taste and the relaxation. "It was close. You had all the right equipment."

Paul's voice became soft, his face pensive. "I feel good about how it all came out. Ken is a lucky man. I try not to get emotional, but I watched my dad die from a farming accident when I was six. Today brought back tough images I've tried to forget."

Liz clutched Paul's arm. "That's awful."

Paul looked down, swirling his wine. "Dad was crushed when a tractor overturned on a steep grade. He died in the emergency room in our small town. I avoided ER in my medical training."

Liz started to say "I'm . . . ," but Paul placed his finger over her lips and shook his head.

"It's okay now. I think I've recovered, but Mom couldn't take farm life without my dad. We don't know where she went or where she is today. Her brother was a terrific father to me, but I have a hole in my heart because both of my parents left me. My Dad didn't have a choice. Mom could have taken me with her and didn't. The worst was being deserted by my own mother."

Liz's sadness grew with Paul's obvious pain. "Then, having your wife leave you for a woman compounded your grief."

"It was a shock, but I'm okay. Since meeting you, this is the best I've felt in months. I can *feel* again." Paul's lips smiled. His eyes remained sad.

Liz spun his stool toward her. "You aren't just okay, you're terrific." She touched her lips to his in a feather kiss. "I am afraid to say much. We only met two days ago, but, I am the happiest I've been in a long time, too."

Paul's lips met hers and melted in a sensual crushing exchange. One of the chefs smiled. The couple clinked their wine glasses in a toast. Then, their ravenous eating interrupted conversation, but Paul's hand on her knee reminded Liz of their evolving emotions.

She leaned back, stomach full, relaxing, letting the chair swallow her. Paul turned the chairs, their knees touching. He held her hands. "I'm exhausted. I have an early meeting at the hospital and then have to fly about an hour and a half to do a bush clinic on the Tulak River. This is a typical clinic day. If you're interested in the village nursing job, it might help you decide."

Liz smiled. "This was a typical day for me. I'm an adrenaline junkie. What time do we leave?"

"I'll pick you up on my way to the hospital about nine."

"That would work. I need to talk to Sharon. Besides, I'm either on foot or taking a taxi. Hitchhiking with you is a lot more fun." She grinned. "I don't usually get kissed by cab drivers."

Chapter 10   In Hiding

A smooth flight and a light clinic schedule made for a relaxing day. Just before Liz and Paul left the clinic to return to Anchorage, a young woman entered complaining of abdominal pain. They evaluated her and found focal right lower quadrant pain.

Liz asked questions related to the patient's menstrual periods and left the bedside to run a pregnancy test with the health aide.

Paul asked the patient more health history questions to evaluate her for a number of possible diagnoses, including appendicitis. "In a woman of childbearing age, there are other serious diagnoses to be considered, including a tubal pregnancy."

Liz returned with the answer—a positive pregnancy test. The woman had missed two menstrual periods. Her positive pregnancy test and pelvic exam revealing a painful mass placed her at high risk for tubal rupture with massive bleeding. Liz started an IV and listened to Paul on the satellite phone talking with the on-call gynecologic surgeon at the Native Hospital. They made arrangements for immediate surgery upon her arrival.

After obtaining confirmation of the airlift schedule, Paul talked with the patient, Liz, and the health aide. "It will take them about two hours to get here. We'll stay here until you're airborne. We need to start a second IV, a backup in case you start bleeding rapidly."

Paul watched Liz as she worked. "Liz, you're famous."

"What do you mean?"

"Dispatch just told me we are on the front page of the Anchorage newspaper, a feature story about the moose crash and saving Ken. For once, they got the details right. He read the part to me about you needling Ken's chest."

The health aide said, "I heard the news on the radio this morning but forgot to ask you about it."

"The dispatcher asked if I'd be safe around you, Liz. He thought you might start sticking needles in me."

Liz looked stern. "Only if you need them." She asked the girl, "Are you doing okay?"

"If I don't move, my belly only hurts a little." She winced as she turned to her side.

The health aide placed a blood pressure cuff on the woman's arm. "It's 90/40. Her heart rate is 90."

Paul increased the woman's IV rate to counter potential blood loss into the abdomen. "Please check them every fifteen minutes and let me know if they change."

By the time the flight team radioed their approach, the patient had received a liter of saline. Her blood pressure had improved to 110/80 before the flight medics packaged her onto the flight stretcher. Paul and Liz helped load her into the transport plane and then climbed in the Maule.

En route to Anchorage, Paul told Liz the newspaper article included an interview and photo of Ken in ICU. "He'd have been in the obituary column without you."

"Without us, you mean. You were the one who flew us there and had all the gear we needed. Anyway, it's satisfying to know our training and experience really did save his life."

"We'll have to pick up a few copies of the paper for your parents, and your friends down in Red Bluff. They'll love it. You tried to escape from flight nursing and failed." Paul laughed.

"They'll be surprised. The feds hadn't entered my mind in the village. Now it's all flooding back."

"You're high profile, Liz. Everyone will recognize your face, now. Anyone with a brain will want you to work with them, including me." He put his arm around her shoulders, bumping the yoke, sending the plane into a turn. "I hope you'll stay in Anchorage even if you decide not to work with me."

Paul leveled the wings.

"I love being with you and feel safe up here. But, we know the druggies are looking for me." Liz frowned. "After that news article, they'll know exactly what I look like."

"They knew before you ever left Red Bluff. Remember, they've been watching you since they lost trust in Jack."

"I'm sure you're right. The day of the memorial service, my apartment was ransacked. Until now, I hadn't connected it. I sold my car to Annie, and then someone destroyed the interior. It all fits together."

Paul checked the fuel gauges. "We left on the flight with about four hours of gas. The tailwind heading home means we have plenty of fuel. I'm glad we don't have head winds to slow us down." He pointed out various landmarks, including two coastal mountains. "Those mountains are Susitna and Little Susitna. The tallest one is also known as Sleeping Lady. The silhouette looks like a woman lying on her back. The smaller elevation to the west is called Little Sue by the locals."

"I noticed the profile when we were flying out. It does look like a woman." Liz scanned the ground. "I love the way the winding river on this side of them spills out into the bay. It makes artistic ripples in the tidal sand."

"That's the Susitna River. I've landed on a sand bar on the river and caught some beautiful salmon."

"You land on sand bars in this?" Liz asked incredulously.

"No, in my Super Cub. I'll take you fishing if you're up for it."

"I'd love to. I used to fish for salmon on the Washington coast with my Dad. He smokes salmon. I had some just before I flew to Anchorage."

"We could do that, too. I have a smoker." Paul circled back, heading toward Susitna, and pushed in the throttle giving the plane more power to climb higher and clear the summit. "I want to show you a runway. Once we cross over the top of Susitna, look down on the smaller mountain. There's a smooth area at the top."

Liz watched the terrain pass below and peered down on Little Sue. "I don't see much of a runway. You could land a chopper, but not a plane."

He turned toward the water. "The landing strip is marked by a white gallon plastic jug."

Liz shook her head. "I think you are kidding. I'm gullible, but I can't believe that."

"The Super Cub is a short takeoff and landing plane. The strip is about 300 feet long, plenty of room to land and a little overrun. The Maule is bigger, and it wouldn't be as safe. I could do it, but only in an emergency."

"If you say so."

"You land and take off the same direction. Downhill. You have only one chance. If you screw up, you'll be in deep kimchi."

"I'd have to get more courage to voluntarily land there." Liz clung to the door frame to stabilize herself as Paul circled low over the dropping terrain.

On the final approach to Merrill Field, Liz's anxiety rose. Her hands were numb and her lips felt tingly—signs of hyperventilation. She'd been taking deep breaths, which could produce that effect. Feeling a little dizzy, she said nothing to Paul to distract him during landing. Liz kept her hands on the yoke and her feet on the rudder pedals while her mind flew off, worrying about what lay ahead.

Would anyone be waiting for them at the airport?

What would she have to do? Face the drug dealers? The killers?

Paul taxied the Maule to parking and cut the engine. They got out. Paul pushed on the tail of the plane to rotate and position the fuselage, so they could push it back into its tie-down area.

"Should we take the medical bags with us to replenish the supplies we used?"

"Not tonight. I don't have an early clinic tomorrow. I usually refuel after each flight. The tanks are low after this flight. I'll fill them in the morning and pick up the bags."

Paul tied special locking knots to hold each wing and the tail secure.

"It's already four-thirty. Do you think Sharon is still at the hospital?"

"She's there till after five most days. I can always reach her. Why?"

"You've been flying me around on company time for two days. I thought I'd tell her I'll be in to sign those papers she talked about."

"Liz, are you staying? Are you serious? Are you going to work with me?"

"If you'll have me with all this damn drug baggage."

"Liz, I've seen you at work. I trust you. I'm excited about having you as a partner."

"You'd better clarify that statement." Liz smiled.

"I mean it any way you'll take it." He swung her around into a kiss that left her breathless.

Her surprise at the spontaneity of his display of happiness at her decision coupled with the sensuous kiss abolished her anxiety. She took her bag from the back of the Maule and closed the door. They walked to Paul's Jeep and turned to find a black SUV with darkened windows roaring up to them. It stopped abruptly, blocking their vehicle. The front doors of the SUV flung open.

Liz gasped.

Drug dealers.

Paul tensed. "Liz, get in the car."

She froze.

Paul took something from the driver door pocket and slid it into his jacket.

Two men exited the SUV and walked in lockstep. The clean-cut duo, dressed in white shirts with button-down collars, blue jeans and dark jackets, looked like twins. The image they projected was unmistakable—the way they walked, the bulge at the hip—and in an instant, Liz realized they were Agents Russell and Forbes.

Paul stood with his left hand on the open Jeep door. "What can I do for you gentlemen?"

Forbes said, "Nothing, Dr. Lasher, we came for Ms. Elliot."

"Where the hell have you been?" Agent Russell demanded of Liz.

Paul glared. "It's none of your damn business."

"We've been looking for you for hours. Two known drug operatives boarded a jet in LA en route here." Agent Russell appeared agitated, sweaty.

Special Agent Forbes scanned the vicinity. "We saw you fly out in the medical plane but lost the GPS track."

Russell glared at Liz. "We've been monitoring the damn aircraft radio traffic all day."

"Excuse me, Agent Russell. You didn't introduce yourselves. Paul, this is Agent Russell, Arizona DEA." She turned to the other man, "And Special Agent Forbes, Anchorage FBI."

Paul said nothing.

"We're in a hurry. The operatives are landing in Anchorage as we speak." Russell glared. "No doubt, they're after Liz."

Forbes explained. "We decided not to set you up, Liz. Too risky."

Paul's face showed relief. He'd been ready for a fight.

"Forbes found a good-looking female agent to serve as your double. I hope you don't mind her wearing your clothes." Russell laughed. "I asked her to wear your red lace bra, but she refused. She looks a lot like you after getting her long blonde hair cut, dyed, and curled."

Liz gasped. "That's awful. She could have worn a wig,"

Agent Russell wiped his forehead. "They would have known it was a fake. They've probably been watching you here, too. Drugs are a real problem in Anchorage and the villages."

"I hope she'll be safe. She's not going to like my clothes. They're not fancy."

Russell quipped, "Your red lace is damn fancy."

Paul clenched his fists. "We need to get moving."

"We vacated the Days Inn. Our men are staked out with Julie, your replacement." The FBI agent offered, "We have a safe place for you in an FBI high-rise condo downtown, Liz."

"No. I want Liz to stay at my house." Paul raised his voice. "They won't find her there."

Liz looked at the agents.

"We were afraid you'd say that," Forbes said. "You could both stay at High Tower."

Paul shook his head.

Forbes asked, "Do you have a weapon, Doc?"

"Yes. I have one in my pocket and others at home."

Agent Russell said, "You're trained to save lives. Some doctors aren't very good at self-defense. Could you kill someone?"

"To save her or myself, yes." Paul was ready to kill the two men who had ambushed them. "Being a doctor wouldn't change that."

Agent Russell looked into the back of Paul's medical plane. "What do you have in those bags? Hey, Forbes, see this? Doc here could be running drugs."

"I am. Legal drugs. Supplies for the clinics, survival gear, and I always carry a weapon in the plane."

Special Agent Forbes tensed, cupping his ear, listening to a small receiver. "They just walked off the flight."

"We're leaving." Paul got in his Jeep.

Liz didn't move. She wanted to hear what the agents were whispering.

Forbes said into a concealed mic, "Okay. Don't lose them."

Paul started the engine and lowered the window as Liz got in.

"We checked you out, Dr. Lasher. It's more problematic for the FBI to stake a guard at your home." Forbes leaned forward and made sure Liz heard. "Agent Burton is already there. You'll be safe with him. He is a big black dude, ex-military sniper, and a Krav Maga expert."

Russell returned to their vehicle, got in, and slammed the door.

Before following him, Special Agent Forbes said, "I hope this will go down as planned today. Burton will let you know when it's over. In the meantime, don't leave your residence for any reason."

Paul followed a perimeter road and headed south toward his home, avoiding downtown. Not sure what they were looking for, they scanned the route. Paul stopped at a red light. "Do you see anybody following us?"

Liz looked back the same instant a vehicle struck them from behind. The impact sent them careening into traffic. She didn't hit the dash, but her seat belt wrenched her right shoulder.

Paul braked, swerving to miss a truck, and screeched to a stop. He turned around to see who had run into them. To his relief, it was a horrified teenage girl driving an old pickup truck rocking with loud rap music. Paul got out and walked back to talk to the driver.

She walked toward him, crying. "I'm so sorry, mister. Are you all right? My dad will kill me for crunching his truck."

"We'll be fine. Are you both okay?"

The teen and her young male passenger assured him they were uninjured.

"Don't worry about the accident." Paul gave the driver his card. "I'll take care of the damage to my car. I'm in a hurry." He bent to examine the front of the pickup. "There's a ding on your bumper. This may not even be a reportable accident. Let your dad decide."

The dumfounded teens looked at each other in disbelief and thanked Paul. He quickly left the intersection to let traffic clear before the Anchorage Police showed up.

Liz watched the pickup disappear from sight. "What a relief. I thought it was going to be drug dealers. I'm paranoid."

"So am I. The thought crossed my mind, too. As they say, 'Just because you're paranoid, doesn't mean they're not out to get you.'" Paul glanced at Liz. "You look pale. Are you okay?"

"I hurt my shoulder when the seat belt caught."

"I hope it's not a fractured clavicle."

"No. I've had worse." Liz ran her fingers along her collarbone. "It's not broken. I'll put some ice on it when we get to your house."

Paul drove over the speed limit on the way home, scanning the roads. Nearing his home, he noted the "For Sale" sign missing from an adjacent house. "Looks like they finally sold the house next door." Paul clicked his garage door opener.

Liz said, "Yeah, to the FBI."

Paul drove into the second-story garage.

Liz looked around as they drove inside and saw no sign of a furtive intruder. "I like this unconventional design. I lived in a second-floor apartment in Red Bluff and found it a pain to climb those stairs with my arms full of groceries."

"The architect did a great job building on this hill. Here, you just walk in to the main level." The garage door rattled down. "I'm exhausted from the vortex we've been in for two days. Now we can lock all the doors and relax."

"Sounds good. I hope Bruno, or whatever his name is, has a quiet night, too."

Paul laughed. "It's Agent Burton. Think of Bert and Ernie. Let's hope he keeps us laughing."

"I hope everything goes well with the covert action tonight." Liz moved to open her car door and leaned back with a yelp. "Dang, this shoulder hurts." She reached over, wincing in pain, and tried to use her left hand to open her door.

"Wait." Paul helped her out.

The entrance to the house opened into a hallway near the kitchen. Liz followed him into the living room. Paul turned on a few lights. "The sun will be down soon."

Liz looked out the floor-to-ceiling windows. The sun sat low on the horizon, casting an orange glow on sparse high clouds. Patches of thin fog skimmed the sea surface on the inlet. "With this immense view looking out, I'm thinking we'd better turn off the lights. Otherwise, we're sitting ducks for anyone interested in taking aim."

"You're right." Paul turned off the lights and disappeared upstairs, returning with two small LED flashlights. He handed one to Liz. "We might need these."

She tucked hers into a jeans pocket. "Thanks. Could I have an ibuprofen and a bag of ice cubes for my shoulder?" Liz rotated her arm. "I think it's just a strain."

Paul directed her to the bathroom cabinet for ibuprofen and handed her a plastic Ziploc bag with ice cubes inside. He opened the refrigerator door and scanned. "I have salad fixings and some fresh mushrooms. I always have a few jars of tomato basil ragu. If we add some sautéed mushrooms, serve it over angel hair pasta, we'll have a quick meal."

"I'll slice the mushrooms if you pour me a glass of wine."

"Deal. Let's have Coppola claret, a great everyday wine. If you don't like it, you know where to find more." He poured two glasses and toasted. "To a quiet night."

"Sure wish I had a police scanner. We could listen to some of the action around town." Paul turned on the television and found a local station. "Let's keep this on mute till it's news time.

"The action we're interested in is covert, so hopefully there'll be nothing on TV about it."

"I'll be back in a few minutes. I want to check the doors and windows to be sure they're all locked."

Paul returned from his survey of the house. The ragu sauce bubbled, and boiling water waited for the pasta. Liz happily sautéed mushrooms, stirring with her left hand. "My shoulder is feeling much better. Wine and ibuprofen are wonder drugs."

Paul darted to the television and clicked it off mute.

Liz joined him.

An attractive blonde reporter flipped back her long hair. "Shots were fired at a local hotel. Ambulances are on scene. The initial report is two dead, one wounded. We'll update you when we have more information."

"Oh, that was helpful," Paul said with sarcasm. "I wish we had more details."

Suddenly, someone pounded on the door and pushed the doorbell repeatedly.

Liz's eyes widened in fear. "Now what?"

"Hide. Go to the wine cellar," Paul whispered. "I'll tell you when it's safe to come out."

Liz grabbed her wine, turned off the stove, and moved silently through the pantry. She descended the circular stairway, closing the trapdoor behind her.

Paul looked through the peephole at a large man dressed in black, leaning on the doorbell.

"Agent Burton?" Paul asked through the closed door.

"Who the hell else would I be?"

Paul opened the door. "Come in." He pulled the man inside and locked the door.

Winded and sweating, Agent Burton removed his cap and used it to wipe his forehead. Burton looked like he had sprinted the distance from the house down the street. In staccato speech, he explained, "The takedown went bad. Three drug operatives showed up and caught us off guard, killed one agent and wounded Julie. Shot her in the chest."

"That's terrible. What do we do now?"

The big man strode to the wall of windows, guided by the low light from the television. He stared out into the darkness. He turned back. "That's not all, Doc. Two Mexicans grabbed the duffel bag and bolted down the one flight of stairs with Agent Russell following them. They jumped into one of our unmarked cars and split, with Russell driving."

"In an FBI car? I don't get it."

"Our guys outside watched it all. They didn't know what the hell was happening. They fired a few shots and took chase, thinking the dealers had kidnapped Russell. They got away."

Paul waited.

Burton took a couple deep breaths and collapsed onto the couch, head in hands. He sat back. "While the medics were starting oxygen and IVs on Julie, she told them the damned DEA agent from Arizona was in on it all the time."

"They won't get far in that car."

"Anchorage police, state troopers, and our guys are looking for them. We have a chopper in the air from a private service on Merrill Field."

Paul asked, "Do you think we're safe here?"

"Probably. They got their loot. I'll stay until I get further orders." Agent Burton paced. "I can't believe this. We looked like a bunch of bumbling idiots."

Paul said, "I hope Julie makes it."

"Forbes said she was bleeding and gasping when the medics closed the ambulance door. They took her to Regional. At least she killed the bastard who shot her."

The two men sat on the couch in front of the television. Paul turned up the volume, hoping they'd get more information.

Burton fumed. "It's a damn fuckup. We have a good department. Now we lost one of our best and Julie might die, too. I wish she'd shot Russell. The damn double agent deserves to die."

"I agree. When someone you thought you could trust gets your friends killed, he deserves the worst."

"I need to look around. We don't want to get caught with our pants down here too. You have three floors, right?"

Paul led him to the stairs.

Burton bounded past him, two steps at a time, returning in minutes. He cruised around the midlevel, and then Paul led him to the stairway to the lower level.

"Where's your girlfriend?"

"She's safe, hiding."

Burton stopped short and took a call using an inconspicuous earpiece and mic. "They've lost 'em. The chopper is up, but our guys are running around like a flock of turkeys. Forbes wants you and your friend in the high-rise security condo."

"We're not leaving. It seems foolhardy to move."

"Don't give me a ration of shit. High Tower is safer. We're afraid they could come lookin' for you. Russell knows Julie was a decoy. Your girlfriend may still be a target, and they might want more than the money."

"She doesn't have anything. It was all in the hotel room."

"He doesn't know that. She's a target, and until they're in custody, you're both at risk."

"Look, Agent, we are not leaving. You're welcome to stay. Dinner is ready. We'd all be safer in here together. In fact, if you station yourself on the upper level, it gives you a 360-degree view, a better view than from the house next door."

"Give me a minute." Burton called someone to explain the situation.

"The boss agrees. He doesn't want you on the street now. I'd love something to eat, but first I want to secure the doors and windows."

Waiting for Agent Burton to return from his rounds, Paul finished cooking dinner.

"This is an interesting layout, Doc. I've never been in a house with such views. The top floor is perfect for me as long as you stay put and don't open any doors or windows. Do you have a security system, like motion detectors, outside?"

"I do, but deer and raccoons kept tripping alarms, so I shut it off."

The big man appeared concerned, his brows drawn together. "I'd like you to turn it on. An alarm would be an advantage."

"I can do it with the flip of a switch. You know, Russell was at Merrill Field when I demanded they let Liz stay with me, so he knows she's here."

"That's what Forbes said. Agent Russell obviously knew drug operatives in Anchorage. They're good at putting tracking devices on people, so Liz might have one on her."

"What a terrible thought. What do the bugs look like?"

"Electronics are so good nowadays, could be anything. They make pens with cameras and tape recorders. Some flash drives have GPS trackers in them. Most of the time, it's a jealous husband tracking his wife, but crooks use them, too."

"There is only one road up here. Can you set up a roadblock?"

"I suggested that. They'll try but might not have the manpower."

Paul lit a jar candle on the coffee table near the TV. "We should eat. The candle provides little light, but with no curtains we can't use the lights. I've never been concerned in the past because the house is so high up. People looking in couldn't see much."

Agent Burton sat on the couch, hunched in front of the television.

Paul disappeared and returned with Liz. He introduced her to Agent Burton. She sat beside him. Paul placed a bowl of pasta, another of sauce, and a large bowl of salad on the table in front of them. The three ate in silence. After eating, Burton excused himself and started upstairs.

Paul called after him, "If you'd like a bottle of cold water or soda, help yourself."

"Thanks for the hospitality. Most of my jobs are not this cushy," Burton said as he backtracked and pulled a bottle of water from the refrigerator. I might come down later for a diet cola."

"I'll be sleeping on the couch here in front of the TV. If you need to get a hold of me, just yell. I'm a light sleeper. Liz will be with me."

Paul walked into the hallway near the garage entry and returned. He called up to Burton, who was still climbing the stairs, "Outside security is engaged. Motion detectors trigger floodlights and generate a beeping sound via the intercom on the wall in your room."

Chapter 11   The Crime Scene

Liz and Paul watched the talking heads and flashing picture on the muted TV, but nothing looked like a police story. Sipping their second glasses of claret, Paul said in an angry whisper, "So here we are, Liz, side by side drinking good wine on a fall evening. As the romantic sun spreads brilliance across the sky in colors you only see in Alaska, we're scared shitless waiting for someone to come and kill us."

"I'm so sorry I got you into this, Paul." She placed her glass on the table and moved to his end of the soft leather couch.

Liz took his glass and placed it safely near hers. "When I was down there alone in the wine cellar, I wanted you to come down, hold me. Make everything all right—make love to me." She peered into his eyes and watched his face, which was shadowed in the candle light.

Paul's angry expression segued to surprise as she slowly pulled loose his shirt and ran her hands over his smooth chest.

His heart pounded. He bent forward and kissed her gently. She moved to straddle him and their lips locked. Her hands unzipped his jeans and slid down, holding him. Paul moaned and moved toward her touch, intensifying their kiss.

Liz pulled away, watching his expression as his soft look turned feral. Another gentle kiss turned voracious.

Paul kissed her neck and tickled her ear with his tongue. "Liz, I want you." He took a deep breath. "Are you teasing me? What if Burton comes downstairs?"

"He won't."

Paul pulled her red shirt loose, moved her bra up, and stroked her small breast, nipple firm. He loosened her jeans and touched a tuft of hair. He hadn't had a woman since his divorce, had never wanted one. Now, he felt he'd never wanted anyone so much.

Clenching Paul, trying to slow down, Liz tried to sort out her sudden passion for him. His kisses and hands overwhelmed her attempt to wait and smothered her fears.

A sudden crash and beeping noise jerked them apart. Burton's heavy steps pounded across the floor above and came down the stairs.

Liz pulled down her shirt and adjusted her clothing. Paul was on his feet, shoving her toward the pantry and the cellar door. She was gone before Burton appeared.

The flickering television and the candle flame cast shadows about the room. Paul pushed his waning erection down and tucked in his shirt. The men met head-on by the kitchen entry. Paul doubted Burton had even seen Liz. It was too dark to see much. Paul ached for her. What a shock, an amazing sensual shock without consummation, and now something chaotic was happening outside. Was someone entering the home?

Liz closed the trapdoor and sat on an iron step near the top to catch her breath, listening and hoping Paul wasn't in danger. She was trying to understand what had happened between them so soon after meeting. Their acceptance of each other in spite of their emotional baggage carried hope, but she was concerned their finding each other was too good to be true.

* * *

Burton and Paul cautiously looked out the second-story window into the back yard. Floodlights illuminated the area. Burton shook his head and eased his hand off the holstered weapon beneath his left arm, hidden by his jacket. He chuckled. "Look at that, Doc. A moose just scared the hell out of us."

A moose cow and her calf meandered into the bushes, leaving behind an overturned umbrella table on the patio and a screaming motion detector.

Paul went to the hallway near the garage door and took his jacket off a wall hook. The heavy pocket told him his handgun was still there. "Had me going, too. It's hell to be scared in your own home. Thanks for being here."

Burton looked around. "Where's Liz?"

"Hiding. She's safe."

Paul settled back on the couch, wanting Burton to go back upstairs quickly. Instead, Burton went downstairs to check everything and asked Paul to reset the alarm system. Then Burton returned and helped himself to a soda. He sat on the couch by Paul. "I'm tired of waiting. I have to check in with Forbes. No news is not always good news." He dialed his cell and waited. "Forbes, what's happening?"

Paul listened to Burton's responses: "She's still in surgery? . . . Good. . . . They still haven't found 'em? . . . We'll be here. . . . Okay."

"So, what's up?" Paul asked.

"Julie's still in surgery. The surgeon thinks she'll survive. No dice on finding Russell and the Mexicans." He got up to go upstairs. "We're to stay here. You might as well try to sleep."

Relieved, Paul's thoughts focused on joining Liz. He stretched out on the couch and waited until Burton was upstairs and all was quiet. After nearly falling asleep, Paul pulled himself from a brain fog and tiptoed to the kitchen. He closed the pantry door behind him and silently made his way down the spiral stairs, closing the trapdoor without a sound.

Paul found Liz asleep on the futon, bathed in flickering candlelight. He leaned against a wine rack and gazed at the beautiful woman who had turned his solitary existence into shocking desire. She lay curled in a fetal position. Paul slipped in beside her and pulled a blanket over them. He couldn't bring himself to awaken her and continue where they'd left off. Paul wanted to protect her from harm and get to know her better in every way. Snuggled against her back, he lay with his eyes open, listening, hoping the night would end well.

* * *

In the cave-like wine cellar, Paul suddenly awakened in blackness. He smelled faint smoke from a candle drowned in wax. He didn't move and held his breath, listening, not sure what had brought him out of an exhausted sleep.

A sharp noise.

A muffled gunshot overhead.

Liz's breathing continued, regular, quiet, sleeping.

Paul sat up, sweeping the floor with his feet, searching for his shoes. He fumbled in his pocket for the flashlight. A sweep of the beam across Liz confirmed she was still asleep.

Paul tucked the blanket around her shoulders. Keeping her safe remained his primary goal.

Footsteps just overhead and a grating noise placed him on higher alert. He hoped they hadn't found the trapdoor.

A door slammed. Harsh voices. Commands. More gunfire. The rattle of a vehicle door opening. His Jeep revved and then he heard it drive away.

Paul pulled out his cell phone, unsure whether it would work in the cellar. The face lit. Sunrise wouldn't occur for about two more hours.

Now what?

Silence in the house. Paul dialed the number Special Agent Forbes had given them.

No connection.

Paul checked the phone. One tiny bar flickered off and on.

A dead zone, they call it. How appropriate. "Can you hear me now?" He sure as hell hoped they could hear him. Paul dialed repeatedly.

A voice finally answered. "Forbes."

Paul whispered "This is Paul Lasher. Gunshots awakened me. I'm hiding out in the house. I don't know what's happening."

"We can't raise Burton."

Paul explained what he had heard.

"Aren't you with Burton? Where are you?"

"Hiding. Can you get someone up here, quick? Someone in my Jeep is probably headed down Highline Drive toward the highway."

The cell went dead.

There was nothing to do but wait. Paul turned out the flashlight and lay down next to Liz, snuggled against her back, wondering how his calm life in the Alaskan bush had become so crazy, yet carried such good fortune.

Liz turned toward him, snuggling her head against his chest. He felt himself wakening inside, wanting her. God, it had been so long since he'd cared for someone.

They awakened to a ringing doorbell. Paul sat up and, in the blackness, found the flashlight and turned it on. He flipped on the wall switch illuminating the room.

Liz rolled her eyes and finger-combed her hair. "I think we have company—again."

Even after the night they'd had, she still looked beautiful.

"Something bad happened." He explained what he'd heard. "I have to get out of here without them knowing where we've been and where you are. You're safe here if no one knows about the cellar. Don't come up."

Paul tiptoed up the stairs, donning his jacket with the weapon in one pocket. He lifted the hatch, stepped into the dark pantry, silently slipped through the kitchen, and peeked into the living room.

Dirty dishes were on the coffee table where he'd left them. He saw overturned chairs, a lamp on the floor, and a muted TV.

The doorbell stopped ringing. Someone rattled the locked door.

A siren drew closer.

Paul went to the door and looked out through the small peephole. He cautiously stepped outside to find four men gathered near the open garage door. Their heads spun toward him as he approached.

The screaming siren cut.

The medic rig's engine roar silenced and stopped, blocking the driveway. Two medics scrambled out and ran to the group. An agent in plain clothes motioned them away. "We need the coroner. Don't go in. It's a crime scene. They're both dead. The big guy is one of our agents. The other, a drug operative."

Special Agent Forbes stomped over to Paul. "Where were you? I'd about given up. What the hell happened here, Lasher?"

"Liz and I were in hiding, asleep, when I heard what might have been a gunshot and called you. That's all I know."

"It's good you were secure or you'd probably be dead like Burton. Shot twice. Once in the chest. Once in the head. He must have confronted them right here. At least he took out one of them." Forbes shook his head in disbelief. "I've lost two men in twenty-four hours. By the way, we didn't see your Jeep on the way up here. I put an APB out on it."

"You haven't found Russell and the two Mexicans?"

"No, but it looks like Burton killed one of them. They must have used the agency car to get here, but we didn't see it, either. Whoever's driving the Jeep could lie low for a while and then take off through Canada on the Highway. We could lose them completely."

Two additional vehicles arrived carrying agents and troopers in plain clothes and a few in uniform. The group of a dozen somber men and women gathered around Forbes for direction. "This is the way it is. I want you all to know this is an FBI case. Our forensics team leads the crime scene investigation. We appreciate the help of the Alaska state troopers. The residence is inside the limits of the Anchorage Borough. I thank the Anchorage Police Department for their assistance in this case."

Forbes scanned the officers. "It's turned into a mess. We all have a lot of explaining to do. What looked like a simple drug takedown in the city ended up killing one of my agents and critically injuring another. Now Burton is dead, too." He gestured to the body on the garage floor.

The group waited in silence.

"I want you to know Agent Julie Myer will probably survive. She's in the ICU with chest tubes after collapsing a lung and nearly bleeding to death. Russell, the DEA double-crossing agent out of Arizona, has not been apprehended. I'd like to take him alive, but don't risk your lives to do it."

A young trooper asked, "How many are we looking for?"

"We don't know. Whoever killed Burton probably made his way here using a tracker concealed on Lasher's vehicle or Liz Elliot's belongings. Whatever they were after was worth killing for."

Paul stood at the edge of the group, listening. Special Agent Forbes caught his eye. "Unfortunately, Dr. Lasher, your home is a crime scene. I'll have someone accompany you. Let us know if there's anything missing. Then you'll have to vacate until the investigation is completed and the building is released."

"So sorry. This is all terrible." Paul hesitated, "You might be interested to know there is survival gear in the Jeep, a sleeping bag, food, and a down jacket."

"Great," Forbes said with sarcasm. "Russell, the goddamned double-crossing killer, is set up for a getaway with survival supplies."

"I'll go in and get Liz. I'm sure she brought her purse from Arizona. Maybe it's bugged like her luggage was."

Forbes looked around, "Where the hell is Liz? She's the one who started all this."

Paul stood tall, protective, resenting the agent's accusatory words. "She's hiding. I'll bring her to your office. When do you want to talk to her?"

"Are you interfering with this investigation?"

"I just offered to bring her in. Obviously, she's still in danger."

"I don't think we'll see any more of Russell. We'll be lucky to make an arrest. Besides, he got the money and the flash drive with all the names of his compatriots, everything he came for, unless he actually wanted to kill Liz for some reason."

"She's very worried about her parents down in Washington State. How will you keep them safe?"

"Her parents are okay. Seattle-based FBI agents have seen no activity near their home. I'm thinking the ones we're after will hightail it back to Arizona and cross into the safety of Mexico."

Paul disappeared and returned with Liz. "Paul told me what happened. I'm so sorry about Burton. We really liked him. I don't see how anyone could have surprised him."

"His death is a terrible loss to this department."

Paul took Liz's arm. "Forbes was saying Russell got away with your duffel bag, the money, and the flash drive."

Liz addressed Forbes. "I saw Russell save the flash drive on his notebook computer when he looked at the data. Did you get a copy?"

"Fortunately, he dropped the computer when escaping from the hotel. We got the data. I have agents processing the names and photos as fast as they can."

Forbes gestured toward the garage. "Sorry about your car, Doc."

"Me, too. I liked my old Jeep, but it doesn't matter. I wish you luck stopping Russell."

Forbes's anger surfaced again. "I wonder if his DEA partners in Arizona know he was working both sides. I don't have any personal contacts in Arizona, so I called the chief down there. But for all we know, he's in on the scheme." Forbes walked back to his men. "Yesterday we received an alert that an Arizona border area ICE agent, active duty on the Immigration Customs Enforcement, was working both sides. Not only helping drug smugglers, but helping illegals cross into the U.S. The ICE agent fingered some DEA employees, so all bets are off. We'll soon know if Russell is on the list."

"Sounds like a huge problem," Liz said. "I lived near the Mexican border for three years and had no idea there was so much corruption and drug smuggling."

"In the past four years, eighty U.S. Border Patrol and DEA agents were convicted of drug offenses." Forbes explained, "We expect it. There is so much money flowing, it's hard to keep people honest."

"How can you trust any of them?" Paul raised his voice. "It's a helluva situation."

"We don't have the manpower to go down there in person." Forbes looked at his cell phone. "Two hours from now, about zero nine hundred, I'd like both you and Liz in the FBI office for a statement."

Paul said, "That doesn't give us much time. Could we make it at ten instead? I have to rent a car and contact the hospital."

"We have to secure this crime scene and move the bodies. Ten is a better time for me, too." Special Agent Forbes stared at his friend's body on the garage floor. "I'll sure miss him. His wife, Geraldine, is pregnant with their first one. I have to go see her before someone else tells her the bad news."

Paul put his arm around Liz. "We enjoyed meeting him. He was thorough and professional. When things went wrong downtown, he came to the door to tell us and suggested we move to High Tower. If we had, he might not be dead."

"Things happen. We have to live with it." Forbes handed Paul his business card with the office address.

Seeing officers stringing yellow crime scene tape around his home flooded Paul with sadness. The serene residence had become the victim of thieves and murderers. He vowed his home would recover its pristine status and provide happy times—with Liz, he hoped.

Chapter 12   Protective Custody

Forensic investigators pored over the interior of Paul's home, examining every surface. They left messy dark powder from dusting for prints. Two men returned from the lower level. One reported to Forbes, "The flood lamps outside are inoperative. A piece of glass is missing from a door window big enough to reach in and unlock the door. They disarmed the security system."

The second said, "It was a silent entry. Burton probably heard nothing until it was too late."

The coroner arrived and took multiple photos even though the FBI team had already taken many. Liz watched him perform limited exams of the bodies sprawled on the garage floor. His photos would help recreate the death scene. Liz thought Burton must have heard something and come to investigate when the intruders were in the garage. What were they looking for?

Paul found Special Agent Forbes enmeshed in discussions with the forensic team. "Could you let me know when your investigation on my property is done? There is a lot of blood to get off the garage floor. I'll need to have the house cleaned top to bottom."

"Sure. It will take us a few days. In the meantime, we'll keep you secure at High Tower until you can return here."

"Do you really think High Tower is safe? I thought I might fly Liz out of town."

"Don't worry. You'll be safe. Surveillance there is easy for us." Forbes gestured toward the city. "Our condo is completely furnished, even with food and liquor. Just pack essentials and a few clothes."

"Okay. Could you find us a ride to a car rental?"

"I'll give you a ride. Let me know when you're ready."

An FBI investigator accompanied Paul to the upstairs bedroom and looked around. "Is this where Burton was on lookout?" The man looked out over the city. "Nice view."

Paul stuffed toiletries and a couple of changes of clothes into a small backpack. Downstairs, he placed his pack by the door with a bag containing four bottles of wine and snacks he'd gathered from the kitchen.

Paul found Liz waiting outside, watching the coroner and forensic team in action. Her head was down, her shoulders drooped. Paul thought she looked like a small, sad child, far away in thought. He wanted to protect her. What was she thinking? She probably blamed herself for the deaths.

Liz turned when she sensed Paul's presence. They sat on the front steps waiting for Forbes, huddled together in silence,

* * *

From the backseat of an FBI sedan concealed by dark windows, blurred scenery whizzed past Paul and Liz during the twenty-minute ride to Anchorage. En route, Special Agent Forbes talked with another agent about the facts of the case and their plans.

Liz tried to reset her brain. There were too many details to absorb. She had to unwind and replay everything at a slower pace to make sense of the situation. She touched Paul's arm to get his attention. "Why do we have to go to the FBI office? They already talked to us."

"Forbes has more questions for you and wants written statements from us. There are a few things we have to do first."

Liz looked down at the outfit she'd worn the day before. "After we rent a car, I have to make a quick stop to buy some clothes. I hadn't planned for this. My clothes are evidence. Too weird to comprehend."

Paul covered his smile. "I shouldn't be laughing, but I think that's an understatement. We'll have time to drive to the hospital and talk to Sharon, then buy a few things for you."

"I only have what I'm wearing. I'll need a toothbrush and a few other things, too."

"No problem."

"I could get everything at Walmart in a few minutes. I'm a quick shopper." She gave Paul a shy smile. "Dang. I doubt if I'll find a duplicate red lace bra and underwear there."

Paul squeezed Liz's thigh, sending an awakening surge through her body. "Believe me, I haven't forgotten Russell's comments. What a jerk! When this is all over, I'll take you shopping to buy whatever you want."

Forbes stopped at the rental agency a few minutes before the business opened.

Liz scanned the area and then opened the door to get out. "Thanks. I'll be glad when this is over. I'm worried about my parents. I think they should fly out east and stay with my dad's brother, where they'll be safe."

Forbes turned to talk to her. "Your parents are fine. No activity around their home but leaving for a while sounds like a good plan."

The second agent got out. "I'll be hanging out with you for the time being as your bodyguard." He held the door for them and then positioned himself in the alcove of an adjacent building with a clear view of the rental agency entrance.

* * *

Paul huddled with Liz. "What do you think about going out to another clinic tomorrow? We'd be safer in the bush. If we leave High Tower early in the morning, we could pick up replacement medical supplies from the hospital on our way to the plane."

"My brain is spinning with visions of death. I like the idea, if Forbes will let us go. I sure hope Julie will be all right."

They entered as soon as the attendant turned the lock. "We need a car and are in a hurry." Paul explained he wanted an all-wheel drive and had previously driven a Toyota Highlander. "It's big enough and has great visibility."

"There's only one on the lot. Dark metallic blue, tinted windows, and a sun roof."

"We'll take it for two weeks, with an option for extension." Paul handed the young man his credit and insurance cards.

Within minutes, the trio headed to Alaska Native Health Center so Paul could explain his absence. He parked in an underground garage and ran up the stairs, leaving Liz in the car with the agent. Paul entered the hall near Sharon's office.

His disheveled appearance and rapid entrance as he streaked to her coffee pot stopped Sharon cold. She said, "I was so worried. I tried to call you after the news report of an unidentified woman struck by gunfire at the hotel where Liz said she was staying."

"It wasn't Liz." Paul dropped into a chair. He drank some coffee and finger-combed his unruly blond hair.

"With us unable to reach you, I was worried you were somehow involved."

"I'll explain everything later. Right now, I'm staying with Liz in an FBI condo. She's under protective custody. The woman who was shot was supposed to be her."

Sharon's face paled. She walked closer, her eyes questioning.

"It's a long story. Don't say a word. If anyone calls for her, you know nothing."

She nodded. "It was a great article about the two of you saving the man in the moose accident. Does it have something to do with that?"

"No. That's a long story, too." He finished the coffee and tossed the cup in the garbage.

Sharon wondered what the heck was going on with this calm, stable doctor who for years had not been this distressed. A few days with a beautiful new nurse, and now he was in trouble with the law. Paul looked terrible.

"I think I'll be able to fly out to the clinic tomorrow, but some supplies will have to be replaced before we leave. I'll call the order in to central processing. Could you have them ready for me to pick up on the way to the airport in the morning?"

"No problem. But why don't you take the day off? I'll cancel the clinic for you."

Paul walked to the door. "I think it will be safer out of town."

"What about Liz? Is she going with you?"

"Yes. She's an amazing nurse, and after our trip yesterday she decided to take the job with me. I am so pleased. She won't be able to come in to HR for a couple days."

"I can't figure you out. If your nurses don't run back to the lower forty-eight, they get shot at. I think you better get a desk job before you get yourself killed."

Paul disappeared down the stairway. He found Liz hunkered down in the Highlander, writing in a small notebook. She unlocked the door.

"What are you writing?"

"A shopping list. My bag with all my gear in it may never return. Do we have time to shop on our way to the FBI office? I'll make it fast." Liz turned and asked the agent. "I really need some things. Could you come in with us?"

"It would be better not to have that kind of exposure. Be hard to keep you safe in a store. You're highly recognizable."

Paul suggested, "If the drug dealers are in town looking for you, I have a baseball hat and sunglasses in my pack you could wear. Not much of a disguise, but you haven't been here long enough for many people to know you."

The agent reminded him, "People will recognize her. You were both on the front page of the paper after the moose crash."

Liz put Paul's cap on and added the sunglasses. "It seems so long ago."

"Yeah, this is Thursday." Paul said, "I could get the things you need if you'd rather wait in the car."

Liz laughed. "Cute. You'd be in there buying toothpaste and tampons for your little girlfriend."

Paul blushed. "It would be a first."

From the back seat, the agent poked Paul's shoulder. "Hey, I didn't think doctors blushed."

Paul said, "I'll get you for that one, Liz."

"Let's go." The agent checked his watch. "It's already nine thirty. Forbes is expecting us at ten."

They blended in with the throngs of shoppers. Liz tossed stuff into a shopping cart: underwear, jeans, shirts, sweaters, hooded sweatshirt, hairbrush, shampoo, lotion, dental and feminine supplies, a pair of dark glasses, and a baseball cap.

The agent pushed the cart. "Sure wish my wife shopped fast. It takes her forever."

Paul said, "It's already Labor Day weekend. This week marks the end of summer. You can't fly in the bush without warm clothing. You need a warm jacket, but I want to go to REI for that and a few other things."

"It seems early to be thinking about winter." Liz tossed in a knit hat. "I'm done."

In the check-out line, Paul noted, "Even in Anchorage we have frost in early September. We'll wake one morning soon with snow on the higher elevations."

The clerk heard his comment. "True. The first snow is *termination dust,* marking the end of summer. I've seen it come in August."

Liz asked Paul. "Do you think I bought enough stuff?"

He laughed. "It should last awhile. I hope this doesn't go on very long." Paul picked up a couple of bags. "I brought some good wine from home. Forbes said someone will shop for us if we need more food."

The three walked back to the rental carrying Liz's purchases.

* * *

The interrogation ended nearly three hours later. While Liz and Paul were in Special Agent Forbes's office, he placed DEA agents in Arizona on speaker phone. They had multiple questions for Liz. Her conclusion, based on their conversation, was Jack Sullivan had led a complex existence, two or even three lives. One intersected heavily with the drug world, something she had not suspected or known anything about. In the end, the investigators seemed convinced she was telling the truth.

Throughout the ordeal, Paul watched her face and mannerisms. Liz sat stoic and answered without emotion. He admired her strength. He'd seen it before in her calm approach to the crash victim and his little boy and to pregnant, abused Sal and her little children. Beneath her unemotional façade was a strong, sensual being.

Paul found nothing about her he didn't like. Her resilience overshadowed a sense of vulnerability she tried to hide. She was alone in a new state, dealing with the loss of friends, false accusations, interrogations by federal agents, a double-crosser, and so many deaths. He knew it wasn't over. He had to protect her, but he hadn't been prepared for what he'd already seen, and he considered an escape to the isolation of the bush with relief.

After signing the interrogation statements, Forbes gave them instructions about the suite at High Tower. He handed them an electronic card keyed for entry to the building and underground parking.

"Don't you think you're being too careful?" Liz asked. "The Mexican who killed Burton is long gone, along with Russell. Isn't this a lot of unnecessary government expense?"

"Liz, Julie is improving, but she came near to dying. It was supposed to be you. We're going to continue in alert mode and protect both you and Julie. Besides, Paul's house is not livable."

Forbes made a short call. A stunning redhead appeared. "Madilyn will accompany you to the unit on the west side of High Tower where you'll be staying. You'll have a view of Cook Inlet, a fireplace, and a stocked refrigerator. We won't let you starve."

"Call me Madi Jo. Let me know if you need anything." She handed them her business card.

Forbes cautioned, "Information on Julie's injuries has been suppressed. If we must answer the press, we decided to handle it by saying an unidentified woman struck in the crossfire is not expected to live and is on life support. Either we'll be fine or a drug dealer will show up to finish Julie off. We'll be ready, and you'll be in High Tower."

"Can I call my parents?" Liz asked.

"Your phone is not secure. It's the one Russell gave you. I need to have it checked out and can return it to you tomorrow. He has the one Jack gave you. You can make a call from one of our office lines before you leave. Paul, do you have a cell with you?"

"I do. So how long do you think this is going to go on?"

"Until we can place Julie safely in hiding, which will be at least a week, or until we're convinced the drug group has given up on trying to get Liz—or we arrest Russell and his friends."

Liz handed her phone to Special Agent Forbes.

"Thanks. We have guards at the condo. Don't leave. If anything changes, I'll call you on Paul's cell. There is a covert action in process in Arizona near the border. I hope it goes better than ours did."

After an emotional and satisfying call with her parents, they followed Madi Jo to underground parking at the condo. She led them to a key-lock elevator that carried them silently to the thirteenth floor of the older building. The doors opened into a foyer dominated by an ornate framed mirror reflecting a fresh flower arrangement on an antique bureau. Their silent footsteps on the soft tan carpet carried them along a sunny hall with rich dark wainscoting.

Liz looked around. "This place looks pricey."

"It's old but recently renovated. Most of the units are private residences. We use ours for FBI dignitaries and as a safe haven for people like you." Madi Jo led them to their suite. "Check and see if your cards are keyed correctly. You shouldn't need them because you are to remain safely inside at all times."

Both cards worked. Paul pushed the door open.

Madi Jo held her hand up, signaling him to wait. She preceded them and quickly swept through the small kitchen area, bathroom, and sleeping alcove. "Everything is in order. I hope you two are friendly. This could be a long wait."

They thanked Madi Jo, closed the door, and walked through the suite together, finding two queen-size beds, a sitting area, and a small kitchen. A small round table with four chairs sat near one of the two large windows. "This is classy. I like the red placemats and bright yellow dishes. The table is set for four. We must be having company."

"Let's hope we see no one." He walked over and double-locked the door. "I've had enough for one day."

Liz sat on an overstuffed love seat angled toward a large window. She stripped off her light jacket, boots, and socks. "I know where I'll be sitting as soon as I get cleaned up." She walked into the bathroom and screamed, "Paul! How could you?"

He ran in to see what was wrong.

"My hair is standing on end! I look like I stuck my finger in a light socket. You didn't tell me how awful I looked, walking around meeting people and shopping. With all the turmoil, I hadn't even combed my hair."

"You look wonderful, striking." He grinned.

"You lie. All I know right now is I need to take a hot shower, brush my teeth, and comb my hair."

"Head on in there. I'll be waiting at the door for my turn."

Liz dug through her Walmart sacks until she found what she needed and then padded into the bathroom and closed the door.

Paul heard the shower running and had visions of joining her.

She emerged from the bathroom enveloped in a cloud of steam and wrapped in an over-sized terry bathrobe, part of the condo amenities. Her hair had become a curly cap. "That was heaven. After days on the run, I felt like I'd never be clean again."

Paul went to her, smelling the fresh scents of soap and coconut shampoo. He wiped a drip of water running down her neck.

His touch sent a chill down her spine.

"I'm next. I poured a glass of wine for each of us. They're on the kitchen counter. I'll be back soon."

While Paul showered, Liz decided she'd better get dressed. The temptation to snuggle together, lost in each other's arms, their clean bodies entangled, shrouded in the luxurious robes . . . would be too much to resist. Clothing would slow things down. How could she be thinking of making love in the midst of this turmoil?

Wine and a plate of cheese and grapes awaited Paul's return. Liz sat in the love seat sipping her wine and gazing out at the landscape she'd viewed from the Captain Cook her first night in town. Five days earlier seemed like weeks ago. The first night had been emotional for her—starting over, not knowing what she would do, with memories of Jack's touch still lingering—and then she was catapulted into the bizarre situation she found herself in today.

Her stomach twisted with anxiety for her parents' safety plus her own and Paul's.

Liz's tension surged as a zing of fear flooded her senses with a visual flash of Burton's body, his brain matter and blood congealed on the garage floor. His black clothing stiff with dark red stains. The other body, an attractive, younger, tan-skinned male, splayed nearby. Their post-mortem blood intermingled in a swirl of surreal art.

Large hands grasped Liz's shoulders.

She gasped and spun around, relieved to see Paul.

"I'm so sorry. I didn't mean to scare you. I thought you heard me come out of the bathroom. That was supposed to be a little squeeze, not an attack."

Liz gripped his hands, pulling them forward to cup her breasts.

Paul edged around the couch and sat beside her. He pulled her into a kiss.

Liz looked into his kind eyes. She slowly swept her hands across his shoulders, pushing the robe off his damp skin. She twirled his blond chest hair as if drawing a picture.

Paul studied her, concerned about her reaction to his shoulder squeeze. He should have known she'd be on edge. He was tense, but she had a calming effect on him. Paul read desire in her eyes. His hands moved beneath her shirt. She was not wearing a bra. He kissed her again, holding back, not wanting to rush. He had to be sure she wanted him.

They had no protection. Pregnancy had always been a negative for him. Now, he didn't care; in fact, he'd be pleased. The thought shocked him. His not wanting children had been an issue in his marriage.

With his patients, he counseled them about safe sex, using protection, avoiding diseases that kept on giving. Right now, he didn't care.

Her fingers moved to his golden pubic hair.

Paul held his breath, his desire increasing.

Liz hesitated. Her life was already out of control. She pulled his robe around his shoulders. "Let's talk about this situation before we do something we'll regret."

Paul wanted her so much.

He understood there were many questions but wanted nothing more than to be with this resilient sensuous woman who was like no one he'd ever met before. "Okay, let's talk." He wrapped himself in his robe and tied the belt. He placed his arm over her shoulder. Paul had never been good at explaining his feelings and hoped he'd do it right this time.

Liz started. "We don't know where we're going or even if we'll be alive tomorrow. If we are, we'll be working together, flying together, side by side. Having a close relationship could be terrific or very complex. Maybe you'll hate me."

"No way. I want you to know I care about you, a lot. But I know what you're saying, Liz. You're in a vulnerable situation."

"Actually, we both are. I care about you, too, but I'm trying to think beyond today. We've been thrown together into an unreal situation. I feel like I'm a character in a movie. The scenes are rushing past so fast, it's difficult to process." Tears welled.

"Liz, we're together. We're safe here. Let's make the best of it. Maybe tomorrow we'll be free, and all this will be behind us."

Liz leaned against Paul. Silently, they looked out at the world. Both wondered what was ahead. A persistent ring from Paul's cell phone penetrated their faraway thoughts. He scrambled to his clothing heaped on the bathroom floor and fumbled to find the phone.

Liz went to his side to listen.

". . . Good. It means we can get out of our luxury prison. What? No. Are they okay? . . . What now? Julie? Is she all right? . . . Okay, when?"

"Who called?"

Paul put his finger to his lips. He pulled her close and turned on a gushing shower to muffle his voice. "Forbes. He talked so fast, it was hard to follow. First, while your parents were out of the house, agents observed two guys entering. They left with a duffel bag and box and then drove off. FBI agents followed. Shots fired. One dead. One in custody. Your parents are fine."

Liz whispered, "I'm so glad they weren't home. Now everyone knows I have nothing to hide and they'll leave us alone."

"Forbes is on his way over here. He's suspicious of everyone after the double-cross. They still haven't located Russell." He turned off the water.

Paul gathered his dirty clothes from the bathroom and stuffed them into his backpack. He carried clean clothing into the bathroom and returned to the living room dressed.

In moments, there was a soft tap on the door. Liz started toward the door.

Paul held up his hand, cautioning her to stay put. He donned his jacket containing the handgun. After looking through the door viewer, he let Forbes enter.

Without a word, Forbes nodded for them to follow him out into the hall. He handed them a piece of paper with a message: *You may not be safe here. Get your belongings and come with me. Don't talk.*

Chapter 13   Bugged

Paul and Liz entered the suite to gather their belongings. He grabbed snacks, wine, and bottled waters from the fridge. They left the suite and followed Special Agent Forbes to the elevator. Once inside and descending, Forbes said, "I don't know who to trust. I received a call on your cell, Liz. They knew you and Paul were staying here at High Tower. They said you still have what they want and will kill you both to get it."

Paul looked at Liz, eyes wide. "What could it be? Do you have anything Jack Sullivan could have bugged?"

The elevator stopped at the parking level. Liz adjusted the small backpack she carried as a purse. "He gave me this."

Special Agent Forbes walked toward his car parked adjacent to Paul's rental. "That has to be it. We got your computer from the hotel room. Forensics found nothing. I have it in my trunk. Did Jack Sullivan use email?"

"Never in my presence. Jack said he used a computer for business only."

"For once, he may have been telling the truth. We got a warrant for his wife's fancy home. A Mexican nanny lives with her. We found a laptop hidden in a crawl space."

Liz clenched her teeth, waiting to hear about more of Jack's deceit.

"His last access on the computer was a few days before he died. The wife acted scared and refused to talk to us without a lawyer."

Paul interrupted Forbes, "This case has so many twists and turns. What next?"

"We'll soon know if they have had a GPS bug on Liz. Follow me to the office. We have some calls and decisions to make."

* * *

The three entered a windowless interrogation room and found two men sitting on folding chairs with their backs against the wall, waiting for them. The younger one was a tall blond guy about Paul's size, and the other was fifty, shorter and dark skinned. Their attire was FBI issue, dark pants and a white shirt, like Special Agent Forbes', who introduced them.

Liz decided they were all business and probably wouldn't appreciate a joke. Their formal demeanor and flat affect revealed no clues. She wanted to do something to lighten the atmosphere but held her tongue.

The men focused on her. One said, "There must be a tracker in your bag that led them to Paul's house and High Tower."

"I wish I'd checked the bag from the beginning." Forbes shook his head. "Somehow it got missed with everything else coming down. It's a big issue and resulted in Burton's death."

"Don't be so hard on yourself." One of the men reminded him, "Russell knew she had it and that it was bugged. He let you overlook the bag on purpose."

Liz inverted the bag and emptied the contents onto the table. "This reminds me of the night you and Russell looked through all the stuff I had in my duffel bag. At least this time it isn't as embarrassing. I don't carry red lingerie in my purse."

"Sorry. We had to do it, Liz," Forbes said apologetically.

Paul raised his eyebrows when she spoke of the lingerie, hoping she'd model it for him someday.

The men gathered around the table and examined Liz's belongings. Forbes scanned the bag using a palm-sized box like the one he'd used in the hotel room. The box emitted a series of high-pitched beeps. Forbes rolled his eyes. "Here we go again."

The agents pulled on latex gloves and took turns examining the soft leather bag, feeling each seam and inside each zippered pocket. "I sure don't feel anything," the tall man said.

Forbes scanned it again, noting it beeped the loudest near the bottom where the two shoulder straps joined each other. The area looked thicker than one might expect just from leather straps. One agent produced a small razor-sharp pocket knife and sliced the stitching. The other said, "Wait. I'll get some tools. Don't want to smudge prints."

With forceps in each hand, the first agent teased the strap open, revealing folded money. He eased out a flattened roll of ten $100 bills with a tiny flat box rolled into the center.

Another object, a funny-looking brass key, slipped out and clinked onto the table.

Liz asked, "Is it a safe deposit key?"

The tall agent picked it up with gloved fingers. "It is. The box is probably a tiny tracker. I'd call this Jack's emergency kit, a tracker to find Liz, and the key to a safe deposit box somewhere. If we can locate the bank and access the contents, it may reveal a lot of answers. Who knows what the box will contain, maybe a lot more money. Airline tickets? Passports?"

The other agent said, "I don't think this is a listening device. It's too small."

Paul leaned forward. "Liz is not going to be a decoy. What do you plan to do now? Place someone back in High Tower and wait for them to come?"

"We'll leave Liz out of it but need your help, Paul. They undoubtedly saw us leave, so I want to have you drive back and walk in with a woman on your arm who looks like Liz. Then we'll sneak you out."

Paul nodded. "That sounds okay. I'm willing."

Forbes continued. "I have agents dressed as maintenance and cleaning personnel on the premises. We could have you dress in maintenance garb and exit unobserved. FBI will be everywhere, waiting for the next step by the drug operatives."

Liz shook her head. "I don't want Paul put at risk."

The agents waited for a response.

Forbes motioned to Liz's belongings. "Could one of you put Liz's stuff back in the pack after photographing everything? I want to reinsert the tracker, money, and key after we make a duplicate." He turned to Liz. "You can keep your wallet, but I need the rest for props. Hopefully, I can get it all back to you in the end." Forbes directed the agents, "Once you have the photos done, process the bug, key, and bills for prints as fast as you can have forensics do it. Call me the minute it's done."

They discussed the details of holding the evidence, reassembling everything including the tracker, and replacing the key with one to a local safe deposit box. "If we lose the bag to them, we may be able to stop them when they try to access the phony bank box."

One agent made a call for forensic help. The other said, "We need to get going on the ID for this key. It may be difficult because the only marking is a number. I would guess it's from a bank in Phoenix near Jack's home."

"I'll get somebody on it right away, but we need to figure out how to keep you safe, Liz." Forbes looked worried. "I didn't tell you. Someone nearly killed Julie at the hospital last night."

Liz squeezed Paul's arm. "How could that happen if there was a guard with her?"

"Our guard took down a woman at Julie's bedside acting as a nurse. He thought she was acting strange, and then she pulled a syringe full of something from her pocket. He had the woman in a choke hold while she tried to stab him with the needle. These people are ruthless."

Paul put his arm around Liz. "I want Liz out of town."

"I'm not going without you, and you're not going back to High Tower." Liz turned to Forbes. "It's foolhardy to ask Paul to go back in there. Everything could backfire again." Liz looked to the other agents for their take on the situation.

The tall one said, "Boss, I could pass for Paul." He stood up near Paul. "See, if we switch clothes, including his baseball hat and Carhartt jacket, I could be his twin."

Forbes studied the two men. "I'm much more comfortable with this plan. It's simple, and you're experienced."

The two tall blond men left the small room and soon returned in each other's clothes. Liz went over and gave the agent a hug and then stepped back, "Oh, I'm sorry, you look so much like Paul. I couldn't help myself."

The guys all laughed.

Liz stood by Paul. "Let's go get something to eat and then get the heck out of Dodge."

Forbes nodded. "Paul, not only are we keeping your clothes, we need the Highlander for your doppelganger to drive."

Paul looked resigned. "We'll need a lift to Peggy's, and then I'll fly Liz out to the bush in my plane where they won't find her."

Forbes nodded. "I'll take you myself. We can't risk either of you being alone till you're airborne. Where will you be staying?"

Paul stiffened. "I'd rather not say."

"Call when you get there so we know you arrive safely." Forbes waited for Paul's response.

"Unfortunately, there isn't good cell phone coverage out there. Nextel is hit and miss."

Forbes pulled a phone from his pocket and handed it to Liz. "Here's your cell phone, the one Russell gave you. Our electronic forensics guys looked it over. It's clean." Forbes turned to Paul. "We'll monitor your aircraft radio transmissions."

Liz asked, "Do you have someone who looks like me to walk in with the agent?"

"Madi Jo is working on it. There may be a local police officer who could do it."

Liz took a deep breath. "Don't tell her what happened to Julie."

* * *

Forbes led Paul and Liz to the secured FBI parking garage. They stopped en route at the Highlander to retrieve Liz's plastic bag of essentials and Paul's backpack from the rental, along with his wine and snacks

From the back seat of the FBI car, hidden from view, Liz watched the passing scenery through downtown as they headed east toward the Chugach Range. Forbes parked at Peggy's Café, a one-story older building painted lavender. The special agent exited the car first and looked around before directing them inside.

Liz got out. "This is not the color I would have chosen for a restaurant."

Paul looked at the building and smiled. "It's a landmark. No one seems to mind the ugly color, probably because the food is so good."

At noon on a Friday, the restaurant was packed. Paul and Forbes ordered burgers, fries, and pie à la mode. After seeing the giant portions brought to other customers, Liz ordered a chicken salad and slice of pie.

A chunky man wearing Levis, a sweater, and an open wool plaid shirt with a pistol bulge on his hip held the door for them as they left. "Hey, Doc, I'm surprised to see you. I saw you fly out this morning way early. Good to see you're back. Did you have trouble?"

"No. Why do you say that?"

"Your medical plane isn't parked next to mine like usual. I thought you were still gone."

Paul frowned. "I'll catch up with you later, Cameron. Good to see you."

In the parking lot Forbes asked, "Who is he?"

"A hunting guide. He's parked his Cessna next to mine for a couple of years. If the hospital plane is gone, it's bad news. I'm the only one who flies it." Paul headed to the car. "Let's get over there."

Paul directed Forbes to his plane's tie-down, passing the parking spot for the medical plane. Paul lowered his window. "I can't believe it. The Maule is gone. Stop."

Paul got out before Forbes came to a stop. He walked to the empty spot where he'd parked the plane.

Forbes and Liz followed him to the plane. "I arrange all the maintenance. I guarantee it's not in the shop. If it's gone, it's been stolen."

Liz walked the perimeter of the tie-down area. She bent down. "There's blood on this rope."

Paul was standing where the left-wing tie-down was located. "Blood on this one, too."

Forbes's eyebrows furrowed. "Goddamned Russell. That's how he disappeared from the face of the earth last night."

Paul looked around, furious. His eyes stopped at a small storage building along the perimeter road. "Hey, there's my Jeep!" He strode toward the vehicle.

Forbes called, "Paul, don't touch it. We have to impound the car and scour it for evidence."

Paul looked inside. "There's blood on the driver's door. The steering wheel is smeared."

Liz walked to the passenger side. "At least there isn't another body."

Forbes shielded the window glare and looked inside through the rear window. "Wrong. There's a body in back."

Liz took a look. Paul placed his arm around her shoulders. "We've all seen too much death. Let's get out of town."

"There were three Latinos at the takedown. Julie killed one at the scene. Russell killed this one. The one dead at Paul's house was killed by either Russell or Burton. Ballistics will tell us which one." Forbes dug in his pocket for his cell phone. "Looks like he wanted to escape with the loot and without a tagalong."

Liz said, "You're right. Remember how he asked what you carried in the Maule when the two of us were talking to you right after we landed? I thought it was odd. What did he think you'd carry in a medical airplane?"

"It's a perfect escape, with medical supplies to treat his wound, survival gear, and a handgun." Forbes punched in a number and kept talking while waiting for an answer.

"I'm so pissed I didn't think about this possibility. A damn search helicopter flew around in circles for hours last night." Forbes paced. "After Russell left your house, he killed this dude and hopped in the plane to head to the lower forty-eight. Fat, dumb and happy. I hope the fucker bled to."

Someone answered Forbes's call. "I have news. Paul, Liz, and I are at Merrill Field. Paul's Jeep is here, covered in blood with a body in the back. The plane he flies to bush clinics is gone." Forbes listened. "So, you found the agency car with bullet holes in it? Shit. We look like the Keystone cops, running everywhere and making fools of ourselves. I'll call the FAA to report the plane missing and trigger both a U.S. and Canadian alert for it. Russell fled the area by air, well supplied."

Forbes nodded, listening. "Okay but get the coroner and forensics over here to impound the Jeep. There's blood all over the tie-down ropes, so we know Russell was wounded." He held the phone away from his mouth. "Paul, what's the tie-down designation?"

"A-46."

"Make Merrill Field tie-down A-46 a crime scene. The Jeep with the body is parked nearby alongside a shed. I'll be here waiting."

Chapter 14   Talkeetna Safety

Paul and Liz waited for Forbes to finish his phone conversation, and then Paul explained, "My Super Cub is close by." He pointed at a yellow plane with large wheels. "I'll fly Liz out of here. If you are monitoring flight traffic, the tail number is Nine One One Delta Romeo. That's an easy one to listen for."

Liz looked at the plane. "How'd you get that number?"

"I bought the plane from a lady ER doctor who had made a special request to the FAA. I kept the tail number. Kind of cool, don't you think?"

Forbes smiled. "I like it. Didn't know you could do that. Sort of like vanity plates for your car."

"I like it, too." Liz pulled their gear from Forbes's car. "Sorry you have to deal with another crime scene."

Forbes straightened. "It's progress. At least we know why we couldn't locate them last night."

* * *

Liz did the walk-around with Paul, watching him check everything. She adjusted a cushion on the back seat and climbed in. Paul helped her untangle the shoulder strap and cautioned her about making sure the waist belt was tight in case they hit turbulence en route, and then he climbed in. "Your visibility won't be great sitting behind me, but once we level out at cruise, it will improve."

Paul put on his headset and handed Liz hers. She tapped the mic and found it working. "Shouldn't we call George and Betsy? It doesn't seem right to literally drop me on them."

"Cell phone coverage is sketchy up there. Besides, I don't want to risk anyone tracking us. Shut your cell phone off. When we get there, we'll use their land line to tell Forbes where to find us if they have news."

"I hope he's not a crook. After all this, who can we trust?"

The plane popped to life on the first try. Paul contacted ground control and taxied to the controlled area, where the tower instructed him to hold his position while a small jet landed. After a few minutes, they received instructions. "Niner One One Delta Romeo, cleared for takeoff. Watch for jet turbulence."

The small plane took off toward the Chugach Range and, as on their first flight, Paul turned toward the north to leave the airport area. Air traffic control asked, "What is your intended direction of flight?"

Paul responded, "Local, scenic, southeast."

Later, Liz keyed the intercom. "You were rather nonspecific. Besides, Talkeetna is north."

"Exactly. We don't know who might be monitoring aircraft radio transmissions."

Liz gazed out the side window en route to Talkeetna, wondering why she and Paul could be so unlucky to be off on yet another misadventure.

It was a scenic and maybe enjoyable route, but they were literally escaping unknown assailants who wanted to kill her. Now the feds had the tracking device and her small backpack for the High Tower stakeout, Liz and Paul would be far away when the drug operatives came for her.

Paul craned his neck to look back at Liz. Because she was sitting directly behind him, he couldn't see her face. "How are you doing? You're awfully quiet back there."

"I'm worried and wishing this expedition was over. I'm glad you can stay in Talkeetna with me. I don't want you in Anchorage, either, but we have to go to work sometime. The way things have been going, we may be hiding out for days."

"Work will wait for us. Sharon will oversee the situation for me. Betsy and George will keep us entertained and well fed, and besides, the dogs will be happy to see you."

The headset-muffled hum of the engine put Liz to sleep.

Later, the sound of Paul's announcement crackling loud in her headset made Liz sit bolt upright. "Talkeetna traffic, Super Cub Nine One One Delta Romeo has an emergency. I'm on a straight-in, landing from the south."

Liz strained to look around Paul's tall frame to see the engine instruments.

The windshield appeared opaque, ice covered.

The weather was too warm for ice!

Prop wash drove rivulets of liquid running off the windshield like rain, spraying onto the fuselage and wing struts.

Oil. Shit, it's oil. Paul said before, without oil the engine could seize and stall.

Liz looked down. They were coming in over trees, low and slow.

In a small voice, she asked, "Paul, are we going to be okay?" She held her breath, not knowing what to expect.

"We'll be safe on the ground in a few feet. We blew a prop seal. The engine is blowing oil." Paul pointed to the gauge. "The engine temperature is rising."

Liz craned her neck to look at the instruments. The oil-saturated windshield provided no forward visibility. She looked out the side window and watched the land rise rapidly. "I trust you." Her trembling fingers gripped her shoulder strap and the window ledge. "We'll be on the ground soon, safe with Betsy and George."

A few seconds later, the wheels squeaked onto the narrow pavement.

Paul stopped at the end of the runway. "The same thing happened to a friend of mine flying into Gulkana in the dead of winter. It was critical because of the weather and the remote area. I think we can get a mechanic to fix this without too much trouble."

Betsy was home with Echo when they stomped up the steps to the door. The dog barked a sharp warning as they approached. After recognizing them, she howled a greeting and wagged her tail. Betsy said, "Come on in. Paul, you look like you're dressed up for church. Are you two out playing hooky from work again?"

"I wish." His tone was angry. "Somebody stole the Maule."

"What? Somebody took it and all your medical supplies? Do you think it was for the drugs?"

"There weren't any narcotics in the plane. We think we know who took it. It's a long story."

Betsy looked at her friends' worried expressions. "What's wrong? You both look like you could use a drink."

"Liz needs a place to hide out. Can she stay here for a few days?"

"I'm delighted. I invited you both to come back. I'm glad it's so soon."

"It's a crazy situation. The FBI wanted Liz out of town. Her life is at risk."

Betsy sat down and studied her young friends, wondering what had happened.

"It looks like a murderer involved in drug trafficking took the plane. He's likely far away by now, but we can't be sure of his associates."

"You better both stay here. There's a queen in the back bedroom if you're friendly or two twins in the middle bedroom if you're not."

Paul smirked and nodded toward the back of the house. He rolled his eyes at Liz, eyes that said, "I want the queen bed, with you in it."

"George isn't home right now. He and Bo drove to Anchorage to buy groceries.

Liz sat down in the kitchen and watched Betsy. "That's a long way to drive for groceries. Maybe we can fly some up for you in the future."

"It would be great for the light stuff, but when you start throwing fifty-pound bags of dog food in, there wouldn't be much room left for you."

"Speaking of flying and carrying gear, we came in my Cub, so we didn't bring much today."

Paul explained more about the investigation and then told her about the prop seal failure.

Betsy listened, speechless. Concern deepened her facial wrinkles that usually crinkled with smiles. "Liz, you poor baby." The elderly woman walked over and placed her arm around Liz's thin shoulders and hugged her. "Here you're a newcomer and they treat you like this. It's just not right. It's not the Alaskan way. You've come to the right place. Echo and I will protect you."

Betsy disappeared into the hallway and returned with a shotgun.

Liz's eyes widened seeing the little old lady cradling a weapon.

Betsy chambered a shell with one smooth move. "George named this after me and taught me how to shoot. 'Betsy' will be right by the door in case someone we don't want to see comes a-callin'. Let's have some coffee." Betsy placed a couple of cups on the table. "Liz, you aren't sayin' much. You must be scared as hell. You'll be safe here with Echo and me."

Paul sat down with Liz.

Betsy filled the cups and placed canned milk in the center of the table. "I have moose stew in the oven. It should be done about six when George said he'd be back."

"Stew sounds delicious." Paul drank most of his coffee and then said, "I need to taxi the plane over to the repair shop after I add a quart of oil. I hope they have a spare prop seal."

Betsy poured more coffee for Liz. "Be sure to come back in time for dinner."

"I'll walk back soon and let you know what's happening." Paul's long fingers squeezed Liz' shoulders. "I don't know how long we'll have to stay."

Betsy hugged Paul. "Hurry back. We love your company. Stay as long as you need to."

Liz looked worried. "You're walking back here, Paul? I don't like you out alone."

"I'll be fine."

"What if something happens here? Can I call you?"

"Turn your cell on in case Forbes tries to call. If you need me, call the shop on the land line and I'll come running." Paul called Forbes to tell him their location before he left. "I'll be back as soon as I can. It's safe. Only Forbes knows we're here."

Liz went to a large window overlooking the runway to watch Paul walk to his little plane, thinking how out of place he appeared, wearing the FBI agent's clothing. She admired his long stride and how he carried himself with confidence. After he added the oil, the prop spun to life with a cough and a puff of smoky exhaust. The engine ran rough but smoothed out before Paul taxied and turned, his prop blast stirring up dust and a swirl of leaves.

The bright yellow plane moved down the narrow taxiway to the only operator, who ran the repair and fuel stop. The man's skills were tested daily by the demands of keeping hardworking bush planes in the air.

Betsy joined Liz at the window. "Things are quiet in Talkeetna. There isn't much going on because we're between seasons. Summertime in Talkeetna draws many tourists to take scenic flights near Denali and Foraker. That's also a busy flying season ferrying mountain climbers to the base camp."

The ladies walked outside after finishing their coffee and stood in the warm fall sun streaming onto the open porch. Echo stood between them. Liz looked around at the beauty of the area, hoping Forbes was trustworthy.

"What do you want to do, Liz?"

"I'm not sure. I feel like I've been in prison for days. Could we take a walk?"

Betsy patted Echo's head. "We are so far from Anchorage, I think it's safe. How could anyone follow you way up here?"

"I can't imagine anyone would know Paul and I are here except the FBI guy." Liz gasped. "I just remembered the feds found a tracking device stitched in an Arizona pack I had with me the last time we were here. The traffickers wanted to get their hands on the pack. The FBI agents have it now and are hoping to lure them in tonight, but I just realized, knowing we visited you before, they might look for us here."

"Luring them in sounds dangerous, but they're pros. I hope they get the bad guys."

"I just hope it goes better than the last one did."

"At first, the feds wanted Paul to help them. I refused. This morning, he exchanged clothes with an agent who looks like him. The agent took his place. I was so relieved."

"I was wondering why Paul was all gussied up when he usually wears blue jeans."

"Echo girl, do you want to go for a swim?"

"Come on. Wear your jacket. There's usually a breeze off the river." The dog wagged her tail and jumped around in a happy dance, and then she ran circles around the women as they walked through town toward the river. "I have a weapon on me," Betsy said. "Just pepper spray, but it's good for both two-legged and four-legged varmints. Echo is our best protection."

"My situation has caused Paul a great deal of inconvenience and anxiety. I hope he doesn't end up hating me."

"Don't believe that for a minute. He's a changed man around you. It's a strong connection. If you ask me, it's love."

Liz smiled. "I think he's amazing."

They passed a few people along the main street. "Most of the tourists are gone." Betsy pointed. "It looks like a couple of them are still here in front of the old country store."

Liz noted a restaurant and a post office. "Is there a hotel in town?"

"The big old white building ahead of us is the inn. They have a few rooms, but I doubt if anyone can actually sleep there. It rocks all summer with live music and dances. It's pretty quiet now except on Friday and Saturday nights."

"Talkeetna's a very small town. How many people actually live here.

"About five hundred, more or less. We'll take you to the inn some time. I like to party. I still have Las Vegas blood running in my old veins."

Liz had to walk quickly to keep up with Betsy and the lanky gray wolf-dog.

Betsy talked as fast as she walked. "This is a nice route through town and then out to the little dirt airstrip by the river. We have two airports, the real Talkeetna Airport by our house and the old Talkeetna Village Strip about a mile from town."

Betsy's wiry body was old but in great shape, like her sharp mind. She showed no sign of breathlessness. "I walk along the old runway and down to the river almost every day to get my exercise and let the dogs swim."

"When we flew in the first time, I noticed you were close to the river. It winds around the town."

"Sometimes, at spring runoff with the snow melting, the water is high, fast, and gray with silt. I don't let the dogs go in then. The old gravel airstrip ends right at the edge of the Talkeetna River, so it isn't far now."

"What a wonderful place to live. Scenic and no crowds."

"There are few cars and no traffic jams except during the Moose Dropping Festival."

"I'm afraid to ask what it is," Liz laughed. "The name conjures up a strange image."

Betsy smiled. "It's a summer dogsled race where the teams take turns pulling an old three-wheeled egg-shaped Isetta car, two wheels in front, one in the back. The course is straight down the middle of Main Street. The dog teams run from one end of town to the other. The one with the best time wins the prize."

"Do they get a trophy?"

"Sort of. It's not what most people would consider a trophy, but it's a memorable prize and a keepsake. Each year it looks a bit different, but basically a few of us collect dry moose nuggets and spray paint them gold. Then we fill up a tall glass vase with them. Winner takes all."

"How funny is that? So, mushers come from all over the area to compete for a jar of moose poop."

"Right. It's fun to watch. Harmless local entertainment until late in the day, when it turns into a drunken brawl."

They walked down the center of the narrow dirt airstrip. A few planes were parked in the tree line paralleling the runway, some barely visible. Liz lagged behind, surveying a stack of inflated rafts and an old fuel truck parked at the town's end along the strip.

When they neared the water, Echo rushed ahead.

Liz caught up to Betsy. "Who uses this strip?"

"Mostly rafters, a few locals, and bush pilots who ferry people to Ruth Glacier the staging area for Denali mountain climbers. A hunting outfitter bought it from the state and closed it to general traffic, but he doesn't care who lands here."

Liz noted, "There isn't much going on today."

"It is quiet now, but it gets busy with fishermen taking float-fishing trips during silver salmon season. Then, after hunting season Talkeetna turns into a ghost town like it is now, until the snow falls."

"Last time, Paul pointed out a moose walking along the river when we were landing."

Betsy nodded. "We have a lot of moose in this area. During the fall, the town fills with hunters. After winter sets in, mushers, cross country skiers, and snow-shoers arrive. I even snowshoe out here to the river in the winter."

Liz said, "Before I came up here, people told me I'd hate the cold after living in the desert. Do you have trouble tolerating the long dark winter?"

"Each season has its challenges. In the summer, it's the mosquitoes. In the winter, it's the short hours of daylight and the cold. After living in Vegas for years, you'd think the long, dark winters would get to me, but they don't. George keeps me busy and happy."

"You and Echo are fit. I'm huffing and puffing to keep up."

"Echo and Bo are strong swimmers."

Liz squatted near the river and swished her hand in the water. "Cold."

Betsy tossed a stick into the slow-moving river. "It doesn't faze the dogs."

Echo leaped in and swam out. She returned, dropped the stick, and shook, spraying the women. After Echo had made many forays into the water, Betsy said, "Echo looks tired but never wants to quit."

The dog came immediately when called. One exuberant shake, and the dog set out a few feet ahead of the women, leading them toward town. They strolled straight down the middle of the runway until a small plane flew over and circled to land. Betsy called Echo and headed for the forest edge with Liz to wait for him to land.

The plane, similar to Paul's Super Cub on tundra tires, bounced a couple of times, stopped short of the end of the runway, and spun around to back-taxi. The pilot waved as he passed them, and then he cut the engine near the fuel shack. After he had passed, Echo took off running and playing. Liz watched the happy dog. "I finally feel relaxed like Echo after this strange, scary week filled with frightful people and happenings. Even though we're in hiding, this is the best I've felt in a very long time."

They walked along in silence, Liz near the forest and Echo in the lead.

The women turned at the sound of footsteps behind them. Liz's heart rate increased.

A man a few yards behind them wearing a gray hooded sweatshirt was walking fast, his head down. The hood partially concealed his face. She whispered, "We must have passed him. Did you see him?" They stepped toward the trees when he was a few feet away, allowing him to pass.

The man approached rapidly.

Liz felt a threat, but believed he was about to pass.

She looked back again, directly into the wild eyes of DEA Agent Russell.

He lunged.

Liz screamed and crumpled to the ground, not moving.

Echo was airborne. Her ferocious teeth locked on Russell's arm.

He dropped his stun gun and fought the dog.

Russell tried to crawl away, groping for another weapon on his hip. Echo pounced, biting his neck. Blood spurted.

Chapter 15   Attack

The large dog's snarling and biting muffled the man's screams. The two rolled on the ground as Russell pushed the dog away, trying to cover his face.

Blood spewed from the man's mouth and neck.

Betsy stepped over Liz's body and checked her pulse. With pepper spray in hand, she grabbed Echo's collar and squeezed the trigger, covering the man's face with the foam-based spray.

The incapacitating orange foam clung to his skin, burning and blinding him. Russell screamed and wheezed, trying to brush the spray off.

The pilot of the plane that had just landed came running when he heard Betsy scream for help. When she realized the young pilot had a gun in his hand, Betsy held Echo close, afraid he might shoot her dog. "Help us." She pointed, "He's a killer."

Betsy picked up the stun gun Echo had dislodged and put it in her pocket. She knelt beside Liz, checking her breathing while continuing to hold Echo, who struggled and growled.

The pilot holstered his gun and stared at the bleeding man, writhing in pain.

Betsy hugged Echo. "My dog saved our lives. That man downed Liz with a stun gun." Echo calmed. "Good girl, good girl. I love you."

Russell rolled over toward Liz. Betsy screamed, "Echo, attack."

The dog lunged, clamping down on Russell's forearm before he could raise the handgun.

Betsy pressed the stun gun to his neck. Russell went limp and dropped the gun. The pilot kicked the handgun away and screamed into his cell phone, "We need help!" He dialed again. "Damn it! I lost the connection." He knelt by Betsy and helped roll Liz to her back.

Betsy checked again for a pulse.

The young pilot waited for an answer. "I sure hope we get better cell coverage up here soon. Is she okay?" He helped Betsy drag Liz's limp form farther away from Russell and turn her to her side.

Echo showed her teeth and approached the pilot.

He backed away with his hands up. "Good girl. Good dog." His phone rang. "Yes. Get a trooper to the old Talkeetna airstrip. Hurry. Attempted murder. Send an ambulance. . . ." He listened. "Damn. Lost 'em again. I hope they heard me."

Echo circled the women, snarling, warning everyone to stay away.

The pilot's phone rang. "Yes. Right. We need a trooper at the old Talkeetna airstrip. We have an injured man and woman. I need an ambulance right away." He ended the call. "Help is on the way."

Relief painted Betsy's face. "I think we better tie the guy up and get rid of his gun before the stun wears off."

Liz lay paralyzed, her eyes wide in fear, unable to speak or move. She stared up at Betsy. Echo licked her face. Liz's increasing awareness of what had happened spiked her fear. A guttural scream came from her pale lips.

Betsy squeezed her hand. "You're going to be all right. Echo saved us." The young bearded pilot squatted by Betsy. "I'm glad I landed when I did. Aren't you George's wife?"

She nodded.

"I'm TJ, Jim and Sally's son." The young man patted down Russell and reached beneath the man's shirt, pulling out a second handgun. Then he pulled a knife strapped to one of Russell's legs. TJ tossed them onto the airstrip, appearing relieved. "I'll get my tie-down ropes." He took off on a run toward his plane.

Echo stood guard over the man on the ground, snapping and snarling in his face until TJ returned.

When Russell began to move, Echo barked and pounced on his chest.

Russell twitched his legs. Groggy and unable to speak, he tried to move. TJ screamed at him, "Stop moving or I'll sic that wolf on you again!"

Agent Russell clumsily moved his hand to his throat. "No. Help me." He mumbled and clutched his bleeding neck.

Betsy ordered, "Echo, get him!"

Echo lunged and crunched down on the man's arm.

Russell stopped moving.

Betsy smiled. "Good girl."

Liz gradually recovered enough to sit up and view the scene. Echo was growling. Russell was lying on his back, unmoving. Blood ran beneath his chin, coloring his gray sweatshirt dark red.

When her foggy brain realized that DEA Agent Russell was lying so close to her, a surge of adrenaline sent Liz into motion, and she tried to crawl away.

Betsy sat on the ground beside her, holding her upright, talking calmly, explaining what had happened.

Liz quivered, uncoordinated.

TJ tied Russell's arms behind his back and then tied his feet to his wrists for good measure.

While Betsy helped Liz scoot farther away from Russell, Echo continued her on- guard behavior, circling the women, snarling. She seemed to sense Russell was less of a risk than he had been but continued her protective behavior.

Just as Betsy was helping Liz stand, George's open Jeep barreled down the airstrip leaving a trail of dust. He jumped out. "What the hell is going on?"

TJ walked over to the approaching man. "Hi, George. Glad you're here. The guy on the ground hit Liz with a stun gun. Betsy and your dog downed him good."

George's voice shook. "How in hell could this happen?"

Betsy explained the situation.

TJ pointed. "He had two handguns and a knife. I threw them over there and got him tied up. Betsy pepper sprayed him good, shocked him with his own stunner. He's bleeding bad from his throat where your dog got him."

George hugged the women and held Liz upright. The large man picked up Liz and carried her to the Jeep. He slid her into the back seat. Betsy got in back with her. George said, "I'll be back in a minute, TJ."

Echo jumped in front beside George. Betsy put an arm around Liz's shoulders, supporting her.

George turned to look at the women in back. "I'm so glad you had Echo and the pepper spray. Who the hell is that guy?"

Liz tested her voice. "It's the DEA agent from Arizona who stole Paul's hospital plane. He's killed a lot of people."

"That explains how he got here, but how did he know you were here?"

Liz raised her head from the seat back. "I don't know, but they use GPS trackers."

Betsy asked George, "How did you know it was us?"

"I didn't. I'd just walked in the door from Anchorage and heard the call for a trooper on the police scanner. I didn't know it was you. I hadn't unloaded the pickup so hopped in the Jeep to see if I could help." George looked around. "Where's Paul?"

"The Super Cub popped a prop seal on their flight from Anchorage. He's at Smitty's getting it fixed."

They drove a short distance in silence. George pulled up in front of an old house at the edge of town and got out. "I'm going to see if Doc Crowley is home since Paul isn't here. Liz needs to have a doctor check her right away. We can let the damn killer die, for all I care."

George strode to the front door of the tiny house with a crooked porch hanging on the front. The door opened. George spoke to an old man. Moments later, George headed back to the Jeep with the overweight white-haired man hobbling behind him. George opened the back door.

Betsy got out and helped Liz move over on the seat.

"Hi, Liz. I'm Dr. Crowley. Could you come inside and let me take a look at you?"

"I'm okay."

Betsy took her arm and pulled her out. "Let him check you over."

The elderly man, who walked like he needed a cane, clung to Liz's arm. She walked slowly to the house with George's arm around her waist.

"I feel like I know you. You're the flight nurse that saved that man in the moose accident. Good work. George told me all about you and Paul. I wouldn't have been much help that day. My gout kicked up. I could hardly move."

The four went inside his home, leaving Echo on guard at the door.

* * *

Liz found herself inside an overstuffed house that smelled of sweet pipe tobacco, much like the rotund doctor. Volumes of books covered an entire wall. She sank into a chair with a caribou pelt draped over the back. The old doctor sat on a footstool in front of her.

Dr. Crowley asked many questions before listening to her heart and lungs and checking her reflexes with a little rubber tomahawk hammer.

She leaned forward and pulled up her shirt, exposing a two-pronged stun mark on her back. "I'm weak and feel weird, but I think I'm fine."

The doctor said to George, "You better get Betsy and Liz home. The trooper will want to talk to them later. I'll drive out to the airstrip and patch up that guy. Lock your doors—maybe there's someone with him."

George drove home. He helped Liz into the house and onto the couch. Betsy covered Liz with a comforter. Echo sat by Liz, her head on Liz's chest, looking at her face.

Liz patted the dog. "Good girl. Thank you. I love you." Liz closed her eyes.

Echo lay on the floor close enough for Liz to rest a hand on the dog. Bo curled up next to Echo.

George wanted to inform Paul in person, but he thought better of leaving the women alone. He used the land line to call Smitty's repair shop.

Liz and Betsy listened to George's side of the conversation. The office put Paul on the phone. First, George asked how the plane repairs were going. "That's good," he said. "So, it'll be ready sometime Tuesday? . . . Can you come back to the house soon? Something has happened. . . . Yes, Liz is all right. . . ."

Liz reached for the phone. "Paul, I'm okay now, but I know where the hospital plane is. I think you'll find it parked in the trees along the old Talkeetna airstrip."

Betsy and George could hear Paul's raised voice.

Liz said, "It's too late. Betsy and I were walking down to the river and Russell attacked me. . . . Yes. . . . A stun gun . . ." Liz shook her head violently. "No, you won't! Troopers are on the way. Russell is tied up, covered with pepper spray, and Echo ripped his neck open. He's not going anywhere."

Liz held the receiver away from her ear.

Paul's tirade continued, so Liz handed the phone back to George.

In a calming voice, George said, "Try to settle down. I'm with the girls, and both dogs are here. Everything will be okay. But I don't want to leave them to pick you up."

George looked at the women and mouthed, "He's hot." To Paul he said, "Maybe you can catch a ride with someone. . . . Okay, we'll be watching for you."

"Paul's walking. He was just about to leave when I called. He's fuming."

Betsy looked out the window and saw Paul jogging along the runway. Nearing the perimeter fence not far from George and Betsy's property, he passed through the gate. The sound of the gate alerted the dogs. His footsteps at the door brought both dogs to their feet. Alert, teeth bared, they flanked George as he approached and opened the door.

Once the dogs saw Paul, their ferocious behavior changed to tail wagging and yips of happiness.

Paul rushed past George and the dogs and sat on the edge of the couch where Liz lay. "Are you all right?"

"I'm scared. I wonder how he found me."

"Why he landed in Talkeetna when he could have flown anywhere is what I want to know." Paul turned to George. "Could I use your landline to call the FBI in Anchorage?"

"Go for it." George brought the phone to Paul.

Paul fished Forbes's business card out of the pocket of the dark FBI trousers he still wore from the clothing exchange that felt like it had happened days ago instead of that morning. Paul dialed. "Madi Jo, I need Forbes right away. . . . No, it can't wait. Get him out of the meeting. I'll hold."

Paul spewed an overview of the incident. "I want to kill that fucker. He used a stun gun on Liz. . . . Yes, she seems okay now. . . , George's wolf-dog did a number on him—for all I know, he's bled to death by now. I hope he has. . . . Hell, no, I won't treat him! The old town doc went out there, and if that's not good enough, so be it. . . . I want to see if the stolen plane is out there. . . . No. I'll stay here and wait for the troopers, but you better get up here and take control. Take a chopper. Forget the medical flight team. You know my feelings. . . ."

Liz admonished Paul. "You're not talking like a doctor. Maybe you should go out and save him. They need him alive to put him on trial. I can help you."

"That jolt must have damaged your brain. I'm sorry to be talking like this, but I almost lost you. It's not going to happen again. In case you hadn't noticed, I love you." With that statement, he kissed Liz gently on the mouth and hugged her so tight she couldn't breathe. When he drew back, tears glistened in his clear blue eyes.

Liz collapsed in his arms and sobbed.

"Come on, you two. The moose stew is ready. Sit at the table." Betsy pulled out a chair and helped Liz sit. "I'll have coffee brewed in a few minutes."

Betsy placed plates and bowls around the table, slinging them as if she might be back dealing cards in Vegas. George followed with silverware and napkins as well as home-made bread. They ate in silence.

Liz startled when the dogs barked after hearing a noise on the porch. George got up and grabbed the shotgun. He pulled back the curtain, peered outside, and then breathed a sigh of relief. He opened the door to a trooper.

"Hey, George. Good to see you. Looks like you were expecting trouble." A tall, dark-haired man in uniform stood at the door holding his wide-brimmed hat in his hand. His eyes fixated on the shotgun.

"We're on edge after today, Harry. Glad you're here. How is that damn drug runner?"

"Agent Russell is still burning from the pepper and is fuming over being taken down by an old woman and her dog."

George chuckled. "Don't cross Betsy. She may be small, but she's tough as nails. That dude learned the hard way."

"He's tied down in the back of the ambulance that just came up from Palmer. They're waiting for the feds to help transport him under guard. I have another trooper guarding him until he's placed in their hands."

"Come on in."

George introduced everyone.

Betsy offered Trooper Harry a meal. He quickly accepted, and after he finished eating, he took statements from the women. The trooper asked Paul to ride back to the airstrip with him to look for the Maule. George remained at home, on guard with the dogs.

* * *

Paul glared at the ambulance, hoping DEA Agent Russell was experiencing pain for what he had done. A second Alaska trooper car was parked near the emergency vehicle. Paul scanned the parked planes while Trooper Harry drove slowly down the center of the airstrip. Small planes sat partway in the trees along the runway. The silver prop of a blue plane protruded from the woods a few yards from where George said Russell had attacked Liz. Paul pointed. "That's it."

Harry stopped. "Let's not touch anything in case the feds want to do evidence collection." The two men walked to the plane. The Alaska Native Medical Center logo confirmed their find.

Paul looked in the pilot-side windows. "There's a laptop computer on the passenger seat. I bet he was tracking Liz's cell phone GPS. Damn, why didn't I think of that? I should have had her keep it turned off."

The trooper said, "We'll find he had internet from one of those special remote cell phone connections. The feds need that computer for forensics."

Paul examined the pilot door. "I see some blood smears in the plane. We thought he was injured in the shoot-out at my house. He left blood stains on the tie-down ropes at Merrill Field. It must have been just a flesh wound if he was able to attack Liz."

Harry looked at the sky. "I hear a helicopter. Let's get my car off the runway." They hopped back in and drove rapidly to the north end, parking near the fuel shack. The men remained in the car until the swirl of dust raised by the chopper settled. Once the main rotors slowed, three men exited the helicopter. They approached Paul and Harry, who stood by the vehicle.

Special Agent Forbes was the first to speak. "I am so pissed off that Russell scammed us again. Someone will have to restrain me when I see him. I'm just glad Liz is all right." Forbes looked around. "Is that piece of shit in the ambulance?"

Harry introduced himself. "Your perp is tied up in the back, handcuffed to the stretcher. A trooper is guarding him."

Forbes clenched his fists. "He killed two of my men and nearly killed another. Russell's in for life if he lives long enough to get sentenced."

"There's a laptop in the Maule." Paul pointed toward the plane. "He must have tracked Liz's cell phone. The possibility that he could have landed here didn't occur to me."

Harry sounded confused. "I don't get it. Why would he come here instead of escaping through Canada?"

Forbes said, "This is another drug connection point. An FBI undercover agent fingered one of the float operators involved in delivering drugs to the villages along the river. Maybe the fishing operation is tied to this whole mess."

"If that's the case, we don't know who the enemy is." Paul looked worried. "I want to get back to George's. If there are more drug connections in Talkeetna, Liz is still a target. They think she has information."

Forbes said, "Wait a minute. I'll go with you to talk to Liz, but I have to ID Russell first. I hate that bastard." He shook his head in disgust and tromped toward the ambulance with the other FBI agents who had flown in.

Harry and Paul heard Forbes yelling at Russell. Forbes returned, flushed and angry. He climbed in the back seat and slammed the door. "I'm leaving my two men here with the trooper to guard the prisoner. I'm taking no chances that he'll escape."

Paul looked back as they drove off toward town and saw the two FBI agents enter the rear of the ambulance. "When can I have the plane back?"

"Not sure. In a day or two. A forensic team should be here soon to check it out. You wouldn't want it now with all the blood inside." Forbes grabbed the trooper's shoulder, "Stop. I need to go back and get the laptop."

Harry made a U-turn and stopped near Paul's clinic plane. Forbes got out and strode to the plane. Paul followed.

Forbes tried the passenger door and found it locked.

Paul pulled open the pilot-side door. "The computer is gone!"

Forbes looked inside. "We need the computer. Where is it? You said the computer was on the passenger seat."

"It was a few minutes ago. This means he had help. Someone took it." Paul looked around.

Forbes said, "That computer contains an information treasure trove for us. The FBI has to get it back."

Harry joined them when he saw they were talking heatedly about something. Hearing their conversation, he suggested, "It could be simple theft. Maybe someone took it when we were distracted by Russell and the commotion of the helicopter landing."

Forbes sounded skeptical. "I only wish it was as simple as that. It's difficult to uncover things in these small communities. Covert activities go on every day. Child molestation and sexual abuse, for instance. My office just uncovered a tragic case in the interior."

Harry said, "I'll contact a few locals I know and put out the word that a plane has been burgled. We want everything back. No questions asked if we get that computer. Okay by you, Forbes?"

"Yes. Let's do a little scouting right now. The sooner, the better. Paul, you check around the plane. I'll go with Harry to see if we can scare up anyone to talk to. Paul, do you have a weapon?"

Paul patted his right jacket pocket.

"Use it if you have to. We'll be back shortly to pick you up and go to George's."

Paul walked toward the medical plane.

Forbes called after him. "You know, for a doctor, you sure seem to get yourself into some strange situations."

"I do."

"By the way, Russell said you left the plane with an empty gas tank. He barely made it in here."

Paul laughed out loud. "The poor thug probably really sweated, hoping he wouldn't bleed to death or disappear in the wilderness like so many aircraft do each year. I wish he had."

"No. We need his testimony, if he'll talk."

Harry said, "Let's get going. I know the kid that happened to land here just before the attack. He grew up in Talkeetna and may be a good source of info. As far as I know, he's never been in trouble, which is saying a lot for these parts."

Forbes and Harry drove over to talk with TJ.

* * *

The plane had carried Paul to many villages through good weather and bad. He walked around the crippled aircraft, defiled by a murderer. Inside, opened medical bags with supplies scattered had been pushed aside to make room for a rumpled sleeping bag. The survival food scavenged. Wrappers scattered the compartment. His handgun, missing. Blood smeared the controls.

He walked away along a narrow path leading through the trees along the airstrip, feeling like he was leaving an old friend. The grassy trail ended after about half a block in an area behind three shanties.

Derelict cars rusted near the dwellings. Weeds grew through the centers of aging discarded tires like potted plants. Paul stood in the forest's shadows searching for a sign of activity around the buildings.

The center structure, less ramshackle than the others, pulsed a heartbeat of music mixed with raucous laughter. The distinctive odor of marijuana drifted from an open window. Paul retreated. He jogged to where Harry and Forbes stood talking with TJ. "Let's take a drive to a shack just beyond that strip of forest. Something's going on. I heard voices worked up over something."

"I know a lot of the people around here. Let's go." Harry headed to his car.

Special Agent Forbes, Trooper Harry, and Paul walked up to a windowless, hand-hewn door. Harry rapped. A young male voice yelled, "Come on in, Aaron. Join the fun!"

Harry swung the door open. They entered to find three teenage boys sitting around a small table sharing weed and staring at porn on a laptop. They looked at the uniformed trooper. "Oh shit! I thought you were my friend Aaron. Ma's gonna kill me. Gino, why'd you bring this computer in here?"

Special Agent Forbes showed his badge. "FBI. What's going on, boys?"

All three of them said, "Nothin'."

Gino spoke, "I found this computer, and when I looked at some of this stuff, it was like nothin' I'd ever seen before. Thought my friends would want to see it."

Forbes's eyes were dark, furious "Where'd you get the computer?"

Thick black hair pulled into a single braid framed Gino's attractive Native face. He examined his hands.

Paul walked to the table to examine the laptop. "The computer on the seat of the plane was a Hewlett Packard."

Forbes walked over to examine the logo. "It's an HP."

Paul felt relief, thinking they had more evidence to convict Russell. "Same type. Looks like it."

Harry, an imposing authority figure in his uniform and standing six feet tall, said, "Gino, I know your folks. 'Fess up. Did you take it from the blue plane parked behind your house along the dirt strip?—Tell the truth and you won't be in trouble. If you lie, I'll see you pay."

Forbes pulled gloves from his pocket before touching the computer.

The teens slid their chairs away from the table, distancing themselves from the scene but curious about what was going on.

A joint burned out on a dish in the center of the table. One teen looked at it longingly.

Forbes examined a card he pulled from the computer. "A phone internet connection." He replaced the card. His fingers clicked across the keyboard, exiting the porn site and scrolling down a list. "The card comes up as a DEA departmental issue. It's definitely Russell's." Forbes summoned Paul. "Look at this. Surveillance software and cell phone tracking. Anybody can get it for a few bucks a month. All you need is an internet connection and you're in business."

"So, you think . . ." Paul stopped when he saw Forbes staring at the screen.

"I don't think, I know. Look at this file. Russell even knew Liz was here before. He tracked her the day of the moose crash. When we met you at Merrill Field, he knew all along." Forbes paused as he scanned a list. "It matches the day she arrived in Anchorage. He followed her everywhere, including today."

Special Agent Forbes said to Gino, "This computer is FBI property and I am taking it with me."

Trooper Harry bent forward staring into Gino's frightened face. "I promised no trouble if you told the truth. Where did you get this?"

The young boys looked at each other. One elbowed his friend. "Tell him."

Gino hung his head. "I went over to watch the chopper land. When I was just lookin' around, I saw the guy who had been sleeping in the plane was gone. I looked into the plane and saw the computer. I hoped we might be able to play games on it. None of us has one." His face flushed. "We got all excited when we found those racy pictures. I was gonna put it back before dark."

Forbes picked up the computer. "Thanks, Gino. You and your friends saved us a lot of trouble. This has already answered some questions for an important FBI investigation."

In the back seat of the trooper's car, Forbes scrolled through computer files en route to George's. Harry pulled over and stopped. "You know, it's illegal not to wear a seat belt, and this warning beep won't stop until you snap it on. It wouldn't look good if we got pulled over." He smiled.

Forbes fastened the belt. "I'm too excited about this computer. God, Paul, I'm glad you found that house and were suspicious about the kids' voices. Today is actually a fortunate day in many ways. We got our killer. Liz is all right, and you got your plane back."

Paul smiled with satisfaction. "I am so glad Betsy zapped Russell. Gave him a taste of his own medicine. He'll never forget this day."

Chapter 16   Safe and In Love

Special Agent Forbes sat at the kitchen table with Betsy and Liz, recording their statements. His cell phone rang just as he finished questioning them. Forbes stepped outside to talk and returned a few minutes later. "Good news. Two men and a woman were captured at High Tower without incident."

He explained that the woman had entered saying she was there to pick up towels to launder and swiped Liz's small backpack by wrapping it in the towels on her way out. Agents let her run down the stairwell to a car waiting in the garage beneath the building. "Our agents ambushed and arrested her. They had already handcuffed and arrested the two men who were waiting. I hope that ends our part of this saga."

George walked Forbes and Harry out to the trooper's car and returned with a big smile. "It's time to celebrate. Betsy, get out the brandy!"

"Okay, pour us some cheer while I finally get the stew on the table. Let's hope it's edible after so many hours in the oven."

George walked to the cabinet near the dogs' candy drawer. His furry friends followed and sat patiently, hoping he'd notice their presence. George gave each dog a butterscotch treat and poured four glasses of brandy.

Liz sat at the table with Paul, feeling safe with her friends. The thud from the low-flying helicopter carrying Forbes back to Anchorage interrupted Liz's thoughts. The familiar sound had been like a heartbeat to Liz, who had flown so many years as a nurse. It had always generated a warm feeling. Now, the repeating thud carried a dull, fading beat like that of a dying heart, reminding her of the dying heartache resulting from Jack's lies and death. She shook off her dark thoughts and looked around the table. Her old life, gone.

A silence swept over her like a dark velvet wing, sheltering her and ending a painful existence laced with lies and deceit. She acknowledged that her life in Arizona had died with Jack. Now she could live again, this time in the wilds of Alaska where she had found a new life.

After dinner, they all retired to the living room, where the television news confirmed the end to a violent story.

Feeling safe and mellow, the four sipped a second glass of brandy and said their goodnights.

* * *

Paul and Liz found their belongings on the queen-size bed in the back bedroom. He closed the door.

Noting their packs on the bed, Liz said, "I think Betsy could tell we like each other."

Before she'd finished speaking, Paul muffled her words with a kiss.

Liz pulled him closer and closer until neither could breathe.

Finally, Paul held her at arms length, his blue eyes smiling. "Nothing is going to stop us tonight, Liz, nothing."

Liz slipped her blouse off, revealing a lacy white bra.

Paul kissed her forehead, her mouth, her neck.

Liz pulled loose his white FBI dress shirt and slowly unfastened the buttons.

Paul stood silently, twirling his fingers through her hair, noting the softness of her dark curls.

Liz unzipped his dress pants, which reminded her for an instant that someone else, wearing his clothes, had done a good job carrying out the arrests.

The rhythmic flash of the airport's rotating beacon swept beams of light through the sheer bedroom curtains. The strobe pulsed in the shadows, followed by abrupt darkness. Just enough light flashed into the room to reveal glimpses of their naked bodies, enough to fan the flames of desire for each other.

Paul pulled Liz down beside him onto the bed, touching her smooth naked skin. He slipped out of his shorts and slid her silky underwear off, letting them fall to the floor. He felt her smooth legs as he snuggled the two of them beneath the down comforter.

Liz faced him, placing her hands on his cheeks, softly feeling his stubble, his neck, and his chest, and pressed her body to his. With her head tucked beneath his chin, lying against his chest, she felt his heartbeat. Liz noted the faint, inviting, clean smell she'd sensed after his morning shower that seemed to have been eons ago.

Paul held her close. "I don't want you to leave, ever. I've been looking for you all my life."

Her breathing became irregular.

Paul looked into her face. The strobe illuminated tears spilling down her cheeks. "Please don't cry. You have been through a lot, lost good friends, endured many changes. You're safe now."

Liz smiled through tears.

Paul kissed salty streaks, glistening in the eerie light.

They turned onto their sides, touching, learning to understand their rapidly evolving feelings for each other. They melted into a union both hoped would survive its chaotic beginning.

* * *

Liz awakened to the smell of bacon and coffee. Morning light beamed into the room. She watched Paul's chest rising and falling rhythmically. His naked body aroused her. Liz slowly moved her hand across his abdomen and down to his pubic hair, inching lower and lower.

Paul groaned and turned to her, smiling. "Is this a dream, a fantasy? We're together and safe."

Liz straddled him, slowly, and slowly allowed him to enter her. They climaxed together instantly, silently. After his erection and their emotions ebbed, they reluctantly parted.

After they used the small bathroom to shower and brush their teeth, Paul dressed in clean jeans and a warm shirt. "I am glad to be in my own clothes again."

"You looked good in the others but too formal for this country. This outfit is better."

Liz tucked a turtleneck into her jeans.

"We're now wearing the uniform of Alaska. We'll fit right in." Paul gave her a kiss and a strength-infusing hug before opening the door.

After breakfast and a second pot of coffee, Liz and Paul walked in the crisp air to check on his plane. Fall foliage in bright colors lined the frosty runway. A shiver slid down Liz's back, reminding her she wasn't in Arizona anymore.

"We need to get you a good winter jacket. The thermometer outside Betsy's kitchen window read twenty-six degrees. That explains the sparkling frost."

The aircraft mechanic said apologetically, "The plane won't be ready until Tuesday. Labor Day weekend, you know. I couldn't get anyone to fly the part up here to me."

Liz smiled at Paul. "That's okay. We'll find something to do."

"Anyway, from what I heard, you both need to relax after yesterday. Good thing TJ flew in when he did."

Paul put his arm around Liz's shoulder. "Word spreads quickly in Talkeetna. I don't think I thanked TJ. If you see him, will you thank him for us?"

"Sure will. He said he didn't do much, though. Betsy and her dog had everything under control."

Liz spent the day with Betsy, harvesting vegetables after the killing frost. They baked bread and seared venison cubes. Betsy placed the meat and fresh vegetables in a crockpot with a few ounces of red wine.

George suggested, "Now that dinner's cooking, let's go for a drive."

They drove out of town in the open Jeep with the older couple in front, Liz and Paul in the back seat, and the dogs sniffing the air from the back. After passing a few deer, an old bull moose, and a tiny red fox along country roads, Liz said, "I feared Bo and Echo would jump out to chase the animals."

"You can never get the wild instinct out of a mix, but these two are very tame. We're their pack now." George glanced back at the dogs. "They know where their food comes from. That makes a big difference. They would have run off when we first got them."

Betsy added, "We trust them after an intense year if training."

Paul wrapped his arm around Liz's narrow shoulders and held her tight as they bounced along. "I'm glad we have our seat belts on today to keep us from being ejected."

George laughed and slowed down a bit.

The dogs curled into balls, wind ruffling their fur. Unless George braked, or some inviting smell brought them to their feet, the dogs remained calm and silent. Liz reached back and petted the animals. "I feel like I'm with my family."

Paul whispered in her ear, "You are."

Upon returning to the house, tired after their long week and the ride in the refreshing cold air, Paul and Liz napped for two hours. When they got up, George, Betsy, and the dogs were asleep. The dogs stirred and joined Liz and Paul in the kitchen, where the couple played double solitaire at the table. Echo lay at Liz's feet. Good smells wafted from the crockpot. Liz whispered, trying not to awaken Betsy and George. "I sure wish they'd wake up, I'm starving."

Chapter 17 Vacation for a Day

Betsy decided Paul and Liz should experience the Talkeetna Inn on a holiday Friday evening. The old white building sat at the end of Main near the end of the airstrip, not far from the attack on Liz. She hoped a jolly time would suppress the surges of anxiety that made her heart pound as they walked toward the inn.

Lively music filtered down the street, energizing the two couples and pulling them inside to the worn wooden floors scarred by years of boot-stomping dances. They threaded their way through the lively crowd to a small table in the back. George ordered a pitcher of beer and filled their glasses with foamy brew. Many of the people greeted George and Betsy.

Paul held up his glass. "Let's drink to calmer times."

Liz clinked all their glasses and sipped. "Last week at this time, I was in Seattle relaxing with my parents. With all that has happened since I arrived here, I feel like I've been watching myself in a movie."

Paul hugged her. "I'm happy the movie ended, and you haven't decided to leave after all you've been through."

"I do like adventure, but this has been too much." Her eyes drifted to the talented singer/guitarist Larry Zarella and the Denali Cooks rock band. They set the crowd in motion. Betsy dragged George out to the dance floor at the start of a lively song.

Paul waited for something slower and a chance to get his arms around Liz.

The raucous music surrounded Liz like a dense Seattle fog. The crowd crushed in, but Paul pulled her out to dance to a love song. He transported her to another place. Trapped in Paul's manly smell, she felt his warmth, his heart, his hand on her waist. She didn't want the song to end, ever. Nor did she want their relationship to end. She made her decision: she was not leaving Alaska.

* * *

Monday afternoon, the FBI released the Maule to a Native Hospital mechanic who flew up to perform a thorough evaluation to be sure the plane had not been damaged. Liz, George, and Paul walked to the old airstrip to talk. Liz stopped on the spot. "This is where Agent Russell stunned me. It was a strange, terrible feeling."

Paul squeezed her hand. "Damn him. The man has no soul. Life in prison is too good for him."

The mechanic lay on the ground beneath the plane. He heard them approach and crawled out. He sat on the ground to talk. "Hi, Doc. The landing gear is damaged. He must have come in here in a bit of a panic, flying on fumes. Both tanks are nearly empty."

"I wondered about that. Liz and I had flown out to a village the day before. We returned too late to refuel."

Liz said, "Right after we landed, Russell and Forbes scared us by showing up like a couple of movie thugs. Russell knew we hadn't refueled. Maybe that's why he flew here instead of heading south over more desolate territory."

Paul knelt down to check the gear. "So, is it flyable?"

"No. The engine is high time, too. I'm going to recommend they find another plane for your clinic."

"Okay. Liz and I will fly back in my plane when the prop seal has been replaced. If I'd known you were coming, I would have had you bring me a seal. We have to wait till the mechanic here gets one tomorrow."

"What's the hurry to get back to Anchorage?"

"I'm in no hurry." Paul put his arm around Liz. "I have to check in with Administration about another plane for my clinic. Maybe they'll purchase that Cessna 180 sitting at Merrill Field with a "For Sale" sign on it."

"Is it the one with wheel skis?"

Paul nodded.

"It's in top shape. The old guy who owned it died during the summer. His daughter wants to sell it and asked me to do the annual inspection on it a couple months ago. If I had the money, I'd buy it myself."

"Put in a word with Administration for that plane when you tell them your thoughts on the Maule."

"I will. Glad you're both all right."

Paul circled the Maule and inspected the bent gear. "I have warm feelings for this plane. I flew it over a lot of rugged terrain. It never failed me. I hope it can be repaired."

Liz suggested, "We could carry some of the medical supplies back to Anchorage with us in the Super Cub."

"We don't have much baggage room. The hospital will arrange for a pickup."

The mechanic heard their conversation. "I drove my truck. Do you want me to deliver your medical stuff to the hospital tomorrow?"

"That would work. I doubt if we'll be flying for a few days anyway."

Chapter 18   Return to Work

En route to Anchorage on Tuesday afternoon, Paul took Liz on a scenic side trip near Denali and flew over Ruth Glacier. The visibility over the blue glacial fields remained good, but bumpy air near the imposing mountain generated impressive turbulence, rocking the wings and making Liz grip her shoulder restraints and tighten her belt.

Paul turned back and followed the Parks Highway. Over Wasilla, he dipped the right wing. "Just off the wing tip, you'll see my friends' place."

"Are those dog houses?"

"With a couple new sets of puppies, he had seventy sled dogs the last time I was out for a visit. He trains race dogs. Some of them have been lead dogs on the Iditarod Dog Sled Race, a thousand brutal miles."

"I can't imagine that much cold and snow."

"They're real Alaskans like Betsy and George. I'll take you out to meet them and the dogs."

"What makes them *real*?"

"You'll know when you meet them. Friendly folk who love the land and the wildlife."

At Merrill Field, Paul landed and taxied to parking.

Liz loosened her seat belt and looked around. "A great flight. No mechanical problems. Clear skies. Calm winds. Beautiful scenery. Everything went right for us for once. And here we are, home and safe on the ground."

"We aren't home yet."

Liz laughed but wondered if an FBI car or drug operatives were racing to stop them. Instead, they found the rented Highlander parked in the Super Cub's designated site. Paul cut the engine. "That was thoughtful of Forbes. We have wheels."

"We need to go to the hospital, so I can sign employment papers. There's probably an orientation I'll have to do before I can join your bush doctoring."

"Don't say *your*. It's ours. I've never worked with anyone on the bush medicine service with skills like yours, or anywhere else, for that matter. I'm not letting you out of my sight."

"Are there any hospital regulations about fraternizing with staff?"

"Who cares?"

"Just asking." Her eyes twinkled back at his.

After Paul had moved the SUV and they'd pushed the plane into its parking place, he sat down on a large tire to call Special Agent Forbes to thank him for delivering the vehicle.

Liz stood by him and listened. She didn't like his report.

"He said Russell is medically stable and will remain in local custody until they decide where the case will be tried. We'll both be called as witnesses, and it may be in Arizona."

"Damn it! I want the whole thing behind us. I never want to go back to the desert!"

Paul was not surprised at her vehemence. She carried demons. The drug trial would only make it worse.

They drove to the hospital, which was located near Merrill Field. An ambulance screamed past them and turned in at the ER entrance. Paul and Liz walked up the stairs to Human Resources, where the receptionist greeted them with enthusiasm. Sharon heard their voices and came out of her office. "Well, look what the cat dragged in. I wondered when we'd see you again."

An urgent overhead page sounded. "Code blue, ER. Code blue, ER."

"Here we go again. We'd better respond." Paul grabbed Liz's arm and led her down the hall. "Follow me. It's just down the corridor from here." They broke into a run.

At the ER, a staff member directed them. "We have a postpartum bleed in shock. OB is busy with a C-section."

Liz and Paul ran into the room. Liz stopped short. "It's Sal. She's unresponsive. Bleeding out."

Under his breath, Paul said, "Shit. What happened?"

Nurses stripped the sheet back, showing a large stain of blood extending from Sal's waist to her knees. "Where's her IV?" Liz asked. "She needs two large-bore IV's stat! Run saline wide open. Get a 100 percent oxygen non-rebreather mask on her. Order six units of O-negative blood stat."

A nurse grabbed IV solution and starter sets. "We have no IV. Medics had trouble getting a line in."

Paul grabbed a pair of gloves and handed another pair to Liz.

Liz directed the nurse. "Massage her abdomen. Massaging her uterus might stimulate it to contract and slow the bleeding."

Paul and Liz searched Sal's pale skin for IV sites. More nurses, a physician, and other staff in scrubs arrived. An ER nurse dragged a large red code cart into the room that was stocked with intubation equipment, drugs, a cardiac monitor, and more intravenous fluids.

An ER doctor elbowed his way to the bedside. "What's the history here? Who knows this woman?"

Paul spieled off Sal's history. "She is about a week postpartum. Liz and I delivered her in Chugalak. She and her baby were admitted last Tuesday." Paul quickly updated the ER doctor as they started IV lines and pumped in saline.

The medic added to the history. "Her sister called 9-1-1. She's had a heavy flow and was weak this morning. Her blood pressure was 70 en route, heart rate 150. I couldn't get a line and so we loaded and ran. We were only three blocks away."

An oxygen mask covered Sal's pale face. She remained unresponsive and was shaking violently. A nurse placed Sal's bed head-down in the Trendelenburg position to improve the blood flow to her brain.

Liz pressed on the patient's carotid artery to check her pulse. "Sal, Sal, can you hear me?" No response. "She's in stage 4 shock, bleeding out. We have to pump blood into her or she'll die. We need O-negative blood and infusers stat."

The ER doctor ordered, "Stat page Lab to run six units of unmatched blood to us! Pump saline until we get the blood."

The oxygen-saturation monitor read 78 percent. The alarm rang a continuous alert.

Liz held out her hand. "I need a scope and tube. She needs to be intubated right away." Liz asked the ER doc, "Do you want me to do this, or are you going to?"

He reached for the tube. "Who the hell are you?"

Liz bagged Sal with high-flow oxygen and looked to Paul for direction.

"Tube her, Liz." He turned to the ER doctor. "She's a skilled flight nurse who works here."

With steady hands and the efficient help of the respiratory therapist, Liz slid the tube in and placed Sal on 100 percent oxygen. The oxygen saturation gradually rose into the mid-80s, and it continued to climb, along with Sal's blood pressure, after she received four units of blood via rapid infuser.

"Where's OB?" Paul asked. "They should be here. We need Sal in the OR stat."

A nurse paged, "OB stat! OB stat! ER! Anesthesia stat! Anesthesia stat! ER!"

The ER doc said, "I bet she has a retained piece of placenta."

Paul looked worried. "Could be. We have to hurry. She'll bleed until they get it out."

The ER doc ordered, "Get 40 units of Pitocin in a liter of saline and start an infusion to help control the bleeding. Type and cross four units of blood and get them up here."

The ER nurse dialed the OR. "We need stat help for a postpartum patient in hemorrhagic shock, probably from a retained placenta."

An anesthesiologist rushed in. "We just finished a C-section in the OB-OR suite on this floor. Help me move her there. Dr. Sherman just finished and will be ready for her in a few minutes."

Four staff members pushed Sal's bed, ventilator, infusers, and monitors to the operating room. On the OR table, with Sal's legs in leg supports, blood flowed freely from her perineal area. Before Paul and Liz left Sal, anesthesia had pumped in more blood replacement, the scrub nurse had set up instruments, and the obstetrical specialist had donned his surgical garb.

Chapter 19   Another ER Crisis

Paul and Liz walked back to Human Resources, where they dropped onto a couch. Sharon sat down with them. "Now you *really* look like something the cat dragged in. What happened?"

"Remember when we delivered that preterm baby girl in the bush clinic the day Liz walked in here last week?"

"It seems so long ago after everything that has happened." Sharon listened as Paul explained the circumstances.

Liz said, "Sal looked terrible today. She's in the OR now."

Paul said, "Liz and the rest of the team saved her. You need to hire Liz fast. Don't let her get away."

"I have the papers ready to sign. I'll be sure you get paid for all the work you've already done. That's the least we can do."

Paul got up from the couch and headed for the door. "While you do the paperwork, I'll go talk to Walt Connelly in Administration about the clinic plane."

"What's wrong with the plane? I heard it was hidden at Talkeetna."

"It suffered a hard landing and is no longer airworthy. Will you alert the scheduler? We can't go until we get another plane."

Liz rested with her head back and eyes closed, reviewing the past week. She waited for Sharon to return with the employment papers.

Sharon touched her arm. "Liz, are you all right?

"I'm fine. Thankfully, we were able to save Sal. I hope her sister is taking good care of the kids, including the newborn."

"You've been through a lot."

"I just need a little time to decompress. Maybe a glass of wine with dinner would help."

Sharon handed her the papers. "I hear Paul knows his wines. He probably has one picked out for you already."

Liz smiled and sat at a table to complete the forms.

Paul returned with a tall man preceded by his oversized belly. He extended a sweaty hand. "Congratulations, girl! Even named the baby after you, I hear. Good job." He held her hand too long. "Sorry you got involved with that whole ER fiasco."

Liz thought he was creepy. She hated being called 'girl.'

"Too bad the Maule is toast. Oh, well, it was insured. We'll find another plane for you." He turned to Liz. "In the meantime, I could show Liz around Anchorage."

Liz cringed at the thought. "Thanks for offer, but Paul has already given me some great sightseeing flights and around town. I think I've brought him more excitement than he expected."

Paul pulled Liz to her feet. "That's all behind us now. I have some plans. Excuse us, Walt. We are going to take advantage of the no-fly status."

The CEO's eyes swept Liz's body as he finished his conversation with Paul. "I'll call you as soon as I have a plane. In the meantime, we could use help with updating bush clinic policies. Check in with the medical staff secretary. You can work from home."

Walt left them with Sharon. "Walt is always focused on the bottom line and women. He's hard to work for."

Paul shrugged. "They pay me on salary, so he doesn't want me sitting around."

Sharon took Liz's papers. "Since your orientation was interrupted by you trip to deliver a baby, you will need to complete the review of basic hospital policies. Sharon gave Liz the internet link. "It's set up online. Since you'll be working in the bush clinic, a lot of it doesn't pertain to you."

Liz wanted to clarify the job. "I assume I'll be hourly. I'm not sure I want to work in ER again."

Paul said, "Let's walk over to ER. I'd like to check on Sal and her kids."

* * *

Nurses directed Paul and Liz to a surgical waiting room, where they found a young woman the image of Sal cradling a fussy baby. When they walked in, Sal's son Billy was sitting at a child's play table. He appeared pensive, absentmindedly rolling a little car back and forth, but he jumped up when he saw them. "Auntie." He pointed to Liz. "She got us an airplane ride with Mom and 'Lisbeth. It was fun."

The woman introduced herself. "Thank you for getting her out of the village. How is she doing?"

A nurse in scrubs with a mask dangling around her neck appeared in the doorway. "Sal has stabilized. You'll be able to visit her about an hour from now in ICU. We'll be moving her there from the recovery room."

Liz asked Paul, "Do you know if there any volunteers that might be able to help with the kids?"

"We're doing fine." Sal's sister assured them. "I have everything the baby needs, but the kids might be hungry. We rushed out of the house so fast, I didn't have time to feed them."

Liz sat down by the kids. "Would you like to go to McDonald's for lunch and Playland?"

The kids cheered. Four-year-old Billy's eyes lit up. He took his little sister's hand. "I told Mom I'd take care of Suzy 'til she comes home."

"You're such a big boy, Billy." Paul patted him on the head and left, returning in a few minutes. "We can borrow car seats. They'll deliver them to the ER entrance. I'll get the car and meet you there."

En route to the ER, Sal's kids skipped along the hall holding Liz's hands. ER staff stopped to talk and thanked Liz for doing a great job when Sal came in critical.

* * *

After devouring Happy Meals, the kids rushed to the play area, in full view of Liz and Paul. Liz said, "I feel safe here, and my burger is good."

"It's a bizarre thought, safe at McDonalds. We'll have to do this more often."

When Paul, Liz and the kids arrived at the hospital, they found Sal's sister sitting in the ICU waiting room with the sleeping baby in her arms. She gave them an update and assured the children their mom was doing well.

Sal's tired eyes lit up when she saw Paul and Liz. She thanked them. Once they were reassured by her progress, they left a contact number and walked back to the rental car. Paul clicked open the doors. "Let's go to the Toyota dealership and see if there's a Highlander in stock."

Liz got in. "That sounds fun. I've never bought a new car."

The salesman offered Paul a good price on a new previous year's model, midnight blue with a skylight, heated seats, GPS, and a good sound system, a lot like the rental. After a call to his bank, Paul confirmed with the salesman that he'd be back in a few hours to pick up the car with a check for the full amount.

Liz admired the car on the showroom floor. "That was way too easy."

"It helps if you know what you want and have the money to buy it. Now let's stop at the FBI office.

Forbes greeted them warmly. "I have news. Would you like some coffee while we talk?"

Paul shook his head. "No, thanks."

Liz explained, "We've both had enough of an adrenaline surge today to keep us going."

"Seriously? I hate to ask what happened this time."

Paul explained.

Forbes shook his head. "You two sure know how to find excitement. What I have to tell you isn't nearly that good, but it's good." He led them to a conference room to talk. They sat at one corner of the polished table.

Liz tensed, hoping it wasn't about going back to Arizona. She really didn't want to think about leaving Alaska for anything.

"First of all, we took the guards off surveillance at Liz's parents' home. We think they're safe after all the arrests."

Liz relaxed. "That *is* good news."

"That's not all. We found a match for the safe deposit key that was stitched into your purse. Another key was taped inside the frame of that Mexican painting you left with your parents. Unfortunately, we destroyed the picture getting it out."

"Thank you. It carried nothing but bad memories."

"The investigation led us to a Phoenix bank near Jack's home."

"What was in the box?" Liz dreaded the response.

"Money, lots of money, close to $500,000, and three passports."

Liz held her breath. Who was Jack planning to run off with?

"The passports were for Jack's wife, whose name is Mary Ramos-Sanchez, and their baby Vinnie. The bleached-blonde woman posing as his wife was actually his sister. The women are in jail. The child's in foster care and will likely go to Mary's mother in Mexico."

"That's an interesting find." Liz leaned back with a great sigh.

Forbes watched Liz's posture soften. "I always believed you, Liz, but this confirms you were a pawn in Jack's hands."

Liz frowned and spit out angry words. "I was so gullible, so dumb."

Paul put his arm around her. "You aren't the only one that makes mistakes. Don't be too hard on yourself. It brought you to Alaska. All the bad stuff is behind you now."

Forbes said, "I wish that were true, Paul. It will probably be a year before this federal case goes to court in Arizona. You'll both be subpoenaed to testify."

"I don't like the idea of going back to Arizona, but I'd love to put that DEA agent in prison for a long time."

"I would recommend both of you make a detailed record of events while they're fresh in your mind. The information will be important, and a year from now, you may not recall the details. You'll be deposed by a lot of lawyers, so you need to keep the dates and data straight."

As they were leaving, Madi Jo appeared with a new leather duffel bag and handed it to Liz.

"What's this?"

"Special Agent Forbes said your bag has to remain in evidence and sent me out to find a replacement."

"That's nice of you. I wouldn't want the old one back."

Forbes heard the conversation and came out of his office, "Liz, I felt bad keeping it, but we have to. Because the guys pawed through all your clothes, we had them cleaned. Your new bag is packed. I'd suggest you leave town while you can."

Madi Jo laughed with Forbes.

Paul took the bag. "She isn't going anywhere without me."

Liz said, "I just signed a contract to work for Native Health in the bush clinics with Paul."

Forbes said, "You're one strong woman. After what you've been through, I thought you might opt for a cabin deep in the woods, far away from dangerous people."

"In spite of all the recent turmoil, I love Alaska. Now we're headed out to buy a new car for Paul. He liked the rented SUV so much he's buying one just like it."

"I liked driving it myself." Forbes added, "Speaking of strong women, I wanted to let you know that Julie is out of the hospital and doing well. She's back walking a couple miles every day, though not jogging yet. She and Charlie said to invite both of you to their wedding. They've set a new date."

Saying they'd be there, Paul and Liz left and drove to the bank, picked up the check, and went to the dealership. Liz drove the new car and followed Paul to the Avis office, where they left the rental behind. Paul slid in beside Liz. "Where do you want to take me?"

"It's only two p.m. and things are calm for once. Let's celebrate."

"How about a drive in the new car out south of town along Turnagain Arm, then home for a home-cooked meal. If the weather is good tomorrow, we could fly out to Wasilla for a visit with Rollie, Vera, and all the dogs?" Paul watched Liz's face for a response. "I wonder if they have any new puppies."

"Let's go. You know I love dogs."

Chapter 20   At Home in Alaska

A restful night and a morning love nest prepared Liz and Paul for a day of play. Paul prepared a filling egg breakfast and brewed strong coffee. They talked about how to spend their day. Paul suggested they fly out to meet his dog musher friends.

"Shouldn't we call them first?"

"They love drop-ins, literally. I usually just circle over the house a couple times. They come out and wave, then meet me at the airstrip about half a mile away."

Liz went out on the deck with her steaming coffee, her breath condensing in the cold air. She looked off to the snowy peaks on the horizon and knew that soon Anchorage would be snowbound, with short winter days.

Paul came out and put his arms around her, pulling her against his firm body.

Liz placed her cup on the table and turned to him, enjoying their closeness and thinking, this is the way a relationship should be. No secrets. No anxiety. Melting together. They had been thrown together just over a week earlier. She'd heard of love at first sight, but this was different. The evolution of their respect for each other had generated trust spiked with sensual chemistry, leaving her feeling warm, comfortable.

She wanted to talk to Paul about immediate plans, such as looking for an apartment for her. It just didn't seem right that she stayed at his house without some sort of discussion.

Paul interrupted her thoughts. "You are far away. I hope I'm part of your dreams."

"You are. I was thinking we should talk about a few important things."

Paul tensed, not knowing what she might be thinking.

Liz leaned against the railing. "Circumstances threw us together. I feel like I've known you forever, but it's only been a few days. I'm afraid to even discuss this because I don't want things to change. I'm afraid bringing it up might jinx us."

Paul led her inside. "It's getting cold out here. Let's build a fire and talk."

They lay on a soft carpet in front of a roaring fire. Paul watched the flames dance in Liz's eyes. He pulled two soft pillows from the couch. With their stockinged feet close to the fire and their heads slightly elevated, they sipped coffee.

Paul lay back to listen. "Okay, shoot. I want to hear what's dancing around in your head. Then, it's my turn."

"So many things are swirling. Are we too close too soon? Should we really work together, when I've heard that can be a very bad idea? Our jobs are meshed. Some couples can handle it, some can't. I have no home. I was too afraid to be alone, and it wasn't really an option. You got stuck with me. I can't believe we found each other this way and will live happily ever after."

Paul's smile revealed beautiful teeth. He kissed Liz's cheek. "I totally understand, but you know what? We'll have a crazy story to tell our kids and your parents. Maybe someday we'll find my mother, so she could meet her grandkids. Liz, I love you and won't let you leave. This is your home, our home." Paul disappeared upstairs and returned dragging the white down comforter behind him.

"It's a little chilly here. This will keep us warm." He pulled the fluffy cover under her chin and then loosened her clothing and helped her slip out of all but her red lace bra and bikini underwear.

Liz wasn't sure if it was the fire, the down cover, or Paul's body warmth, but she was definitely warm. In fact, she was hot when she felt his strong hand stroking her thigh and between her legs.

"Your skin is smooth, like satin. I love touching you. This is how I wanted it to be with us. I pictured you in front of the fire, naked and warm."

Liz turned toward him, removing his jeans, shirt, everything. She took her time. She pushed back the comforter to admire him. The fire crackled, sending flickers of strange images across their skin. "I like to look at you. Seeing and feeling you aroused lights my fire."

Paul leaned back, comfortable, exposed, ready. "We have all day."

Liz kissed his lips, his chin, his neck. She twirled his blond pubic hair and held him back as she slowly removed her underwear.

Paul took deep breaths, maintaining control. He unfastened the red lace bra and leaned forward to kiss her breasts, bringing her closer to climax. She backed away, catching her breath. As her breathing slowed, his lips found hers, his tongue probing as his hands slowly pulled her hips down on him. Their bodies pulsed, melting in a feral fusion that gradually ebbed. She lay on him, satisfied and safe. They fell into an exhausted sleep beneath the white cloud of silky down with the fire crackling.

They awakened in the early afternoon and dressed. Paul talked about homey topics—puppies, Liz's parents, going to Seattle for a visit, and attending Julie's wedding in November.

Liz carried the comforter back upstairs to their bed. She fluffed her hair and returned.

He watched her walk down the open stairway. She looked beautiful.

She asked, "Is there anything to eat?"

"Bread, cheese, wine, and fruit. That's about it."

"Perfect."

They sat on the couch, watching the flickering fire and eating. "After wine, I can't fly, but after just one glass, I'm fine to drive. What would you think about going out to meet the dog mushers?"

"Great. Should we call?"

"I usually don't. They like drop-ins, just like George and Betsy in Talkeetna. I just circle over the house a couple times. They come outside and wave, then meet me at the airstrip about half a mile away. Since we're driving, though, I'll see if they are up for a visit."

Paul called. He talked a few minutes. "We're on. Betsy already called Vera and filled her in on you. They're delighted we are coming out."

They sipped coffee on their hour drive to Wasilla, enjoying the luxury of the new car and just being together. Liz liked the leather seats but wanted to sit closer to Paul than the seats allowed. She reached over and ran her fingers through his hair.

Paul rested his hand on her thigh, enjoying her presence.

The divided highway to Eagle River made driving easy, but the scenic route narrowed to two lanes when it curved around the saltwater tidal bay of Knik Arm and wound its way north. At mile 63½, Paul turned in to a narrow quarter-mile driveway that circled around a small square house.

A dog on the porch howled a greeting when they drove in. Rollie came out and opened the passenger door. "This must be Liz. Glad you came. We haven't seen Paul in weeks. George and Betsy told us you've been hiding out with them."

Liz got out and petted the blue-eyed Husky mix that followed Rollie. "Who is this?"

"That's Sugar. You'll see why I named her that. We love the little mutt. She's only six weeks old. We chose her for our new house dog. Punkin, our other house dog, had her trained in a couple of days. Vera babies them."

Vera walked down the three steps to meet them. "Paul, I'm so glad you brought Liz out to meet us. Come on in. I hope you're hungry."

After fresh rolls and chicken soup, Rollie took Liz and Paul on a walk to visit the dogs. Dozens of barking dogs stopped barking immediately when Rollie rapped a stick on the side of a fifty-five-gallon barrel. "That's my signal to them to hush up. I feed them two hot meals a day, a slurry of meat and fish over dry dog food. They love it."

"I want to bring Liz back out after it snows and take her mushing."

"Just let me know when." Rollie turned to Liz, "I'll give you a few lessons and then you can each take a three-dog team on the trail behind the house."

Rollie walked back toward the house. "Liz, come over here and meet Sugar's brothers and sisters. You might want to take one home." He winked at Paul.

Liz followed Rollie to a large pen confining a bundle of puppies rolling around and climbing over a beautiful female with a masked face and blue eyes. Liz held each of the little dogs and petted their docile mother. A small female with dark facial markings stared at Liz with blue eyes and snuggled into her neck.

Liz reluctantly placed the puppy back with the litter.

Rollie invited them in for coffee and apple pie before they headed home. They ended up staying for another hour. Rollie was interested in all the details of the drug arrests. Vera shared her bread and pie recipes with Liz.

On the way home, Liz read over the recipes. "My mom is a good cook. I guess I better learn. You have some great friends, and I love those puppies."

"They are wonderful, in their late 70s and full of life. I often spend weekends with them. I think they stay young because they are always ready to party and have so many young friends."

"It's getting dark early."

"Wait till the winter months. In December, the sun comes up about ten and goes down about three. That doesn't leave much time for flying to the clinics. Sometimes weeks go by before we can fly out to see patients."

"What do you do then?"

"I work at the hospital in the Family Medicine Clinic. I'm sure they'll find a place for you, too. Do you still think you'd like to work in ER?"

"Not if the same doctors are there. I'll check with Sharon and see what her thoughts are."

Chapter 21   Little Sleeping Lady

Paul and Liz snuggled beneath the soft comforter and slept. In the morning, they awakened enmeshed. The house was enshrouded by fog. They unwound and showered together, enjoying each other, feeling as though they had flown far away on a special vacation.

Liz stood naked, looking out the windows. "This fog reminds me of growing up in the mountains north of Seattle. We had a lot of fog in the fall and winter. I rather like being hidden in clouds. No one can see us, and we can't see out."

"But I can see you. I like what I see and feel. You make me very happy, content to be anywhere as long as we're together."

Liz went to Paul and wrapped her arms around his naked waist. "The feeling is mutual. We could stay here all day or do a little more exploring." They went back to bed until noon.

The fog had dissipated when they awakened again. Paul stood at the window. "This looks like a glorious day."

"I love the view, but aren't you concerned someone might see you?"

"We are too high up. No one can see in. Come look."

Liz joined him.

"See. The world is far below."

Liz looked into the distance. We had snow last night."

"You're right. That's termination dust. Winter is coming. This is the perfect time to land on Little Mount Susitna. Much later and we'll have to wait till next year."

Paul kissed Liz. "I am a very lucky man to have a star drop from the sky and land right here beside me."

"Flattery will get you everywhere."

"Dress warm. We'll make a lunch and coffee for a picnic."

Paul drove to Merrill Field. They were soon airborne in his small plane with tundra tires, perfect for rough terrain and off-field landings. On takeoff, the Chugach Range glistened white against a clear blue sky. The ground cover, flushed red after the hard frost, looked afire.

Turning west, they flew across Cook Inlet toward Mount Susitna, the sleeping lady mountain. "Is this where you showed me the little mountain airstrip?"

"It is. The view is spectacular. I want you to see it up close, to share something I love with you."

They flew along the lower slope of Little Mount Susitna. He circled, dipping a wing. "Look, there are three black bears. I think they see us."

Liz said, "Don't land close to them. I've had enough excitement."

"Don't worry. We'll be on the top. They're a couple miles downhill."

Paul circled and lined the Super Cub up at the summit marked with the plastic bottle at the beginning of the landing area. Liz asked, "Are you sure you want to do this?"

"I'm sure. You'll like it."

Paul landed downhill and braked abruptly on touchdown. The wheels bumped over the tundra as the plane ran out of smooth landing area and finally came to a stop.

Liz hung on, not at all sure landing on the top of a mountain was a good idea. Then, Paul turned and taxied back up the sloped landing area to a flatter spot at the top.

He cut the motor and got out.

Liz followed. "She gazed off into the distance. This is breathtaking. Anchorage looks like a tiny village down there."

"Look toward the west. It's the Alaska Range. Sometime, we'll fly close to Mount Spur, one of the white peaks. It's an active volcano spewing sulfur fumes and steam."

Paul reached behind the back seat into the small baggage area. He pulled out a blanket and their lunch. The wind rustled low bushes.

"Let's walk over to where the terrain drops off."

Liz pulled up her hood and followed him.

They sat on boulders at the edge of the earth, looking down on the world below. Their coffee and breath steamed in the cold air. In the distance, miles away over Turnagain Arm, dark clouds moved toward them as they munched their sandwiches.

Paul followed her eyes. "I see the snow clouds, too. We may have white ground in Anchorage by morning. Are you worried about the coming weather?"

"A little."

"We have plenty of time to get back. Even if we're marooned here, we have survival gear."

"I'm more worried about the bears coming to visit."

"We've seen worse than a few bears recently."

Liz smiled, "I see why you like it here. This is the most beautiful, peaceful place I've ever been."

"I brought you here for a very special reason. I have never shared this spot with anyone. I come here to gather my thoughts, to look at the world, to look at the stars, to think about the future."

Paul hugged her. "You're trembling. Are you cold?"

"I'm chilly, but mostly overcome . . ." Liz placed her hands over her eyes and struggled to hold back tears. ". . . with emotion."

"Don't cry, Liz. You are safe now. No one can hurt you. We're alone on top of the world, and no one knows we're here." He gave her a crushing hug. "Drink some more of your hot coffee. I'll be right back."

Liz watched Paul's long legs carry him back to the plane. He returned with two sleeping bags, pulled them free from their stuff bags, and placed one on the ground behind her, the other around their shoulders. "We can keep each other warm."

He lay back against the silky down bag and pulled her down on him, kissing as they fell, their lips and bodies on fire in spite of the cold. His fingers traced her lips and then loosened her bra. He pulled up her yellow polar fleece shirt to suckle her breast and glimpsed red lace. His eyes widened. "You wore this for me again?"

Liz smiled, "You seemed to like it." She kissed him hard and, seeing a sensual bulge, loosened his jeans.

The icy wind touch Paul's naked skin as the down sleeping bag fell away, exposing both of them to falling snow.

Liz mounted him, feeling him slip inside. She pushed down accepting him fully for an instant.

He didn't move, afraid it would end too soon.

She inched her body above him repeatedly until their moist surfaces barely touched, then suddenly plunged. Paul's gasp and rhythmic release triggered her orgasm. In unison, under a darkening icy cloud, they became one. Stars brightened the sky as the lovers slowly recovered and pulled the down sleeping bag up to shield them from the cold.

Paul kissed her. "I love you, Lizzie. I want to spend the rest of my life with you."

That is what she had waited for Jack to say, so long ago. Hatred for Jack and love for Paul twisted in her heart.

"Liz, we're an awesome pair." Paul kissed her tears.

"Aren't you afraid of me?"

"No. You're soft with children and puppies, but tough when you need to be. I've watched you. I respect you. I've never felt this kind of love before. I have never wanted kids, but you make me want a child. Will you marry me?"

Liz didn't have to consider his question. "I will. I love you, Paul."

His lips parted in a smile. "Wonderful. I have another question. How do you feel about adoption?"

Her muscles tensed. "Adoption? Why? Can't you have kids?"

Paul's eyes smiled. "I thought we should start with a puppy. I asked Rollie to save Sugar's little sister for you."

Liz screamed in delight. "When can we get her?"

"I'll tell you all about it, but we better pack up and get airborne before we get stuck here."

By the time they reached Anchorage, a light snow sparkled in the streetlights and covered the grass with diamonds.

THE END

Questions and Topics for Discussion

1. What did you like best about *Alaska Flight*?

2. How did the Alaskan setting enhance the story's intrigue and Liz's escape from her problems?

3. Does Liz's struggle with grief and deception ring true with your life experiences? What other themes did the author explore through Liz's relationship with Paul?

4. How did Paul help Liz adjust to dramatic changes in her life? How did he resolve his own life crises with Liz's help?

5. Was the ending satisfying?

6. Would you read another romantic thriller by this author?

Afterword

Thank you for reading *ALASKA FLIGHT.* I hope you enjoyed it. If you did:

- Tell your friends and help others find this book by writing a review:
  https://www.amazon.com/dp/B079CZ5NHK
- Like my Facebook page:
  http://www.facebook.com/betty.kuffel
- Check out my author pages on: Amazon
  https://www.amazon.com/-/e/B007BI6SW8
- Visit my website: http://bettykuffel.com

I enjoy discussing my novels with book club readers. If your group is interested in talking with me during your discussion of *ALASKA FLIGHT*, please contact me at: MontanaSunriseBooks@gmail.com to schedule a time to Skype.

I look forward to hearing from you.

Betty

Acknowledgements

Many thanks to Dennis Foley and friends in Authors of the Flathead who have been instrumental in guiding my writing over years. Special thanks to my enthusiastic critique members, Debbie Burke, Deborah Epperson, Marie Martin, Phyllis Quatman, Susan Purvis and Ann Coleman, who remain generous with their time and skills.

I also thank my husband Tom for his support, help with cover design and publication formatting. Thanks to Bev Erickson and Blue Heron Loft for the final cover. Copy editor Kathy McKay provided excellent advice for improving the final manuscript.

About the Author

Betty Kuffel, MD

Dr. Kuffel is a retired ER physician who lives in Montana. Medical and wilderness experiences, flying, dog sled racing in Alaska and surviving a plane crash in the mountains of Idaho fuel her writing.

Made in the USA
San Bernardino, CA
25 June 2018